THE HARVEST OF SOULS

THE HARVEST OF SOULS

ARTILECT WAR BOOK THREE

A.W. CROSS

GLORY BOX PRESS

The Harvest of Souls

Copyright © 2018 by A.W. Cross

Published by Glory Box Press
British Columbia, Canada.
gloryboxpress@gmail.com

First edition, 2018
Epub edition

ISBN 978-1-7751787-6-7

Cover design by germancreative
Interior design and formatting by Glory Box Press
Editing by Danielle Fine, www.daniellefine.com

FOR H.

01
AILITH

In the dream, I made my way through the waving grass of the emerald sea once more. The blades were brittle and dry, their tips crusted with the salt that permeated the air and seasoned my lips. My steps were slow and resolute—no longer the flight of a child.

I couldn't see them, but I knew they were there, the others like me. Both human and machine, an involuntary legacy turned harbinger. And behind them, a cast of ninety-nine following in formation, heartless and soulless and free. Their power at my back was both soothing and terrifying, an expanse of dark water that was, for the moment, calm, but in whose depths lurked a terrible power.

The hundredth walked beside me, his hand clutching

1

mine. His face was set, looking only forward, although the tightness with which he gripped my hand betrayed…what, I wasn't sure. He didn't feel like I did, but he knew fear. And grief.

My companions wound silently through the houses we passed. The buildings were ghosts, their presence only suggested by faint outlines and the berth we gave them. Both familiar and unfamiliar, their bricks were built from our collective memories, pressed into clay and mortar.

Had the houses always been there? I couldn't remember.

Wraiths lingered in the doorways of these ghost-houses, trapped forever in their own time. Even through the veil of ages, they felt our presence, their pale fingers scrabbling against the lintel as their empty eyes searched for us, their voiceless mouths trembling in uncertainty. Further on, the buildings multiplied as epochs overlapped, and the specters' gazes sharpened in accusation, epithets dripping from their tongues as their fingers tried to press the vision of us into their rheumy eyes.

From under those fingers, a sickly network of corruption spread, a viscous blackness creeping over their cheeks in spindly lines. As we passed them, they fell, a lament on their lips that cracked like thunder in our ears. The shadow-homes crumbled, some into ash, others into dust, all into ruin.

Doubles rose where the originals had fallen, one after the other in rapid succession, like an echo. They saw only each other, for we'd faded beyond their sight into obscurity. As we brushed past, they merely made a sign of protection against us, and were consoled.

Beyond the shades, the tree rose from a blanket of mist, solitary still in the green expanse. It was a familiar comfort, and something more, something that, for the first time, I almost understood. Our march toward it remained steady, deliberate. We all had a purpose there that must be fulfilled.

As our legion advanced on the tree, fear surged inside me that we would crush it. How could we not? We were an army, and one not of flesh. But there was no way to stem the tide—I couldn't even stop the rhythm of my own feet. I had made our decision, and there was no going back.

Moments before impact, we split like a wave against rock, flowing around the immense trunk until we'd encompassed it. It was then that we stopped, and that I finally understood our purpose: protect the tree. Defend it at all costs, for at its base was the means of our survival, the only means left to us on the path we'd taken. We faced outward as one, our anticipation pointed and unpitying.

A sudden sigh stirred the air, and the earth shifted beneath our feet, heralding a blur of bodies as the red mist descended. Its bloody condensation gathered on the leaves of the tree and rained down on us, gods and monsters meeting at last.

The harvest had begun.

Would your answer change if this question wasn't merely philosophical? What if you were faced with the very real decision to choose between living the truth, no matter how bleak, or staying within your perceived existence? Could you be happy either way? Knowing that you had the choice to live in comfort and didn't for the sake of truth? Or living in comfort knowing that it could be called, by some, a lie?

—Cindra, Letter to Omega

02

AILITH

My skin giving way under the rough bark was what finally roused me. I awoke with a start, the salt from my dream still clinging to my lips. In front of me stretched the vastness of the Pacific Ocean, the horizon dotted with mottled smudges of green and brown—other tiny islands like ours, adrift in the glassy green expanse. The sharp sting of abraded skin pierced the fog of my reverie, and the red mist dissipated. Reaching back, I traced the graze the thick ridges of the colossal oak had left on my shoulder. My fingertips came away red, and I wiped them on the grass, the blood soaking into the salt-crusted blades and making them supple again.

The dream left behind a hollow burning in my chest. Tor hadn't been waiting for me by the tree, nor had he walked with me. He'd *always* been part of the dream before.

What did it mean? Was he dead? Lost to us forever?

The last time I'd seen him was shortly before my death, his eyes wide and wild as he clawed his way toward me, dragging his frozen legs uselessly behind him. We'd searched for him every day for six weeks, following the route we believed he'd planned to take. But that was the plan he'd made *before* my death. Or at least, what he'd thought was my death. After my body was destroyed by Umbra, the artificial intelligence that had grown like a cancer within the body of another cyborg, Tor had left as he'd promised he would and missed the resurrection of my consciousness into another body.

I didn't know what he would do in his grief, but he wasn't the type of man to give up. He'd lived through the Artilect War, surviving the death of his mother and everyone he'd known as he guarded me for the five years I'd slept. For all that time we'd been bonded, and whether he knew of my survival or not, that connection remained.

I just had to find him.

The first few days after my resurrection, I'd tried to use my talent for linking to the minds of other cyborgs to pinpoint his location, but the power in my new body simply wasn't developed enough to find his thread. Or so I hoped. I couldn't bear the alternatives—that our link had somehow been broken, or worse, that his thread had gone forever dark, joining the others who'd died.

Or what if my ability's simply incompatible with Eire's?

When I'd been brought back to life in Eire's body, our abilities had combined. She'd been able to see the past, but so far, I'd found her power elusive. Unable to use either skill, I'd been forced to stop looking for Tor, resigned to waiting for my strength to return.

But today, with the changes in my dream, I had to know.

Should I ask Pax?

I kept hoping he would say if he knew what had happened to Tor, one way or the other, but so far, he'd been silent. He sat below me now on the pebble beach, his head bowed as he busily threaded bait onto a hook. He refused to use live bait—he thought it was cruel—but he did love fresh fish.

I'd expected the ocean to be in the same state as the rest of the province—barren of people, quietly hostile, populated with new plants and animals driven down from the freezing north—but it was warmer here by the sea, and there were signs that recovery from the sun-blocking ash of the firestorms might not be out of the question. Even the old oak trees for which the island had been famous still stood, their leaves yet supple as they clung stubbornly to the branches.

Before the war, Helene Island had been a determinedly rustic destination for tourists who wanted to spend their days technology-free, hiking, golfing, and watching for orcas. Despite the perfect climate, the imposed limitations on technology had kept the former population of the island very small. Less than three hundred people had lived in a tiny village of clustered houses, spending their days accommodating tourists, making wine from the island's vineyard, and fishing in the famed salmon creeks. When we'd arrived, the population had disappeared completely, and so we'd adopted it as our home, moving into the village and laying down our roots.

The salmon creeks were now bare, but Pax persevered in the ocean and, every few days, was rewarded. It was this quiet determination that had enabled him not only to survive his torture at the hands of the Terrans, but endure the particular demands of his unique ability. He'd changed the course of our lives many times with his capacity to see forward through time, calculating present variables to predict all future outcomes and try to keep us alive. Since settling on the island, Pax had spent increasing amounts of time traveling down these future paths, sometimes for days, so it was good to see him here now, in the present.

And it was all thanks to Fane, our resident artilect and the cause of the Artilect War. Fane's presence brought many complications, not the least of which was his creator's desire to get him back at any cost. He'd left with us when we escaped our compound, and it wouldn't be long before they tracked us down.

Their looming shadow was the only sure thing in our lives, and the wait kept us restless, our nerves taut. Even now, Oliver, the former CSIS agent-turned-cyborg who'd given up his pure humanity for his mission, scanned the tiny island for signs we'd been discovered; our safety was his prime concern. He'd come a long way since his time as a selfish, narcissistic god. Part of the reason for that was Cindra.

She'd embraced a romantic relationship with Oliver after Asche, her former boyfriend, had rejected her, afraid of what she'd become and blaming her for the death of his family. On the beach below, she laughed up into Oliver's face, a golden feather glinting in her hair. She'd found it the day we'd left the compound, and she'd kept it to honor her grandmother and remember her lost people. Like Pax, she showed no outward signs of the torture she'd endured. She'd even started recording our story, although I didn't know who she thought would ever read it.

They were all occupied, quiet. Now was the time. A warm breeze caressed my face, the scent of withered olive trees and salt carried on the air. I settled back onto the bark of my oak tree, ignoring the pain, and closed my eyes. One by one, the threads connecting me to the others flared into existence. I held my breath, afraid they would vanish. When I was sure they were sturdy, I searched for Tor's thread, halfheartedly at first, not wanting to know the truth.

There. Before, the thread that connected me to him had blazed, solid and unwavering. Now it was dark, almost black. Which meant—

Wait. A flicker. I'm sure of it. I—

The day I first saw him was in Goldnesse. He was so tall and strong, with dark, shining hair and serious eyes. I thought he was the most beautiful man I'd ever seen. I still do. He didn't smile easily, and I decided that would become my new goal: to make this mysterious man smile. I believed that, in the moment he smiled, he would finally see me.

—Love, Grace

03
TOR

Why am I in the dark? Why can't I move? Where is—

I couldn't feel my body. My mind was foggy, my thoughts incomplete.

Have I been drugged? What happened?

Ailith. Callum, his thin, ravaged body shaking as Umbra forced him to lift the rock over his head before bringing it down on Ailith's skull.

Blood. So much blood.

I'd…covered her. Carried her back. I'd given her to Cindra, to the others. And then in the commotion, while they were distracted, I'd left.

Why can't I feel my body?

I'd gone back to find Umbra, to make sure she was dead. And if she wasn't, I was going to make her pay for what she'd done. But by the time I'd gotten back, Callum was gone. I'd stared at the blood clotting in the dust and known what I had to do.

I'd intended to go west. To find an island, like Ailith and I had planned.

And I had gone west. I'd stayed in the trees, crossing out into the open only when absolutely necessary. I hadn't lit fires. I'd eaten whatever I managed to catch, whatever was unlucky enough to cross my path, raw. I hadn't bothered trying to keep warm. The cold wouldn't kill me, unfortunately. Just put me to sleep.

But I hadn't covered my tracks. I hadn't been quiet.

I'd stumbled blindly, thrashing through the brush. I hadn't cared. I just needed to reach the coast, to get as far away from what had happened as possible.

I'd stood at the edge of a ravine. The murky sky had pressed down on me, encouraged me, while the stones below waited to embrace me. I'd taken one step then another… I'd passed out. I slept. Dreamed.

Three days later, I turned back. I needed to find the others. I shouldn't have left them. She wouldn't have. What had happened to them? Had they escaped? Had they been taken with the compound? How had I been so selfish?

How did I get here? I can't remember.

I turned back…

I…

A thin strip of light appeared a few inches from my face.

Making him smile was harder than I'd thought it would be—he'd been through a lot during the war and losing a parent would hit anyone hard. But I persevered, and today, for the first time, he looked me in the eyes and a smile touched his lips. It was only the ghost of a smile, but still, it's a start. And now that I've seen what his smile could be, I can't stop thinking about his mouth.

—Love, Grace

04

AILITH

"He's alive," I whispered. Hearing the words aloud made them true. "He's alive," I said again, louder this time. Then I screamed it.

Startled, the others turned toward me. The bait fell from Pax's hands and floated out to sea.

"Ailith?" Fane called. "Are you all right?"

I ran down the narrow path that led to the beach. At the bottom, I fell, my hands and knees crushing painfully against the unforgiving rocks and shards of shell.

"Ailith, what happened to your back? It's bleeding." Fane pulled at the spotted fabric clinging to my skin. As I pushed his hand away, Cindra and Oliver abandoned the kelp basket Cindra had been weaving and hurried over.

"He's alive."

"Who's alive?" Cindra knelt and put her hand on my

shoulder. She scanned me subtly, using her ability to see if I was okay.

"Tor. Tor is alive."

Her shoulders slumped. "Ailith—" she began.

"He is, Cindra. I *know* he is."

"How do you know? We all want him to be alive, but—"

"I found his thread. It was dark, only a flicker, but I followed it. It worked this time. There's something wrong with him… But he's alive."

The others exchanged glances, and I knew what they would be thinking if I stepped into their heads. *She's finally lost it. Maybe for good this time.*

"If he was, we would've found each other by now," Cindra said gently.

"Why do you all think he's dead? He could just be lost, trying to find us the way we tried to find him. This isn't the only island—there are a lot of them. Maybe we're on the wrong one. Maybe he's on one of *those* islands," I said, gesturing wildly to the smudges of brown and green in the distance. "Maybe he's sitting on one of those, waiting for us to find him, or maybe he's waiting for a sign from us so he knows where we are."

"Ailith, when he brought you back… What happened, it was too much for him. He—"

"Why didn't you make him stay? Why did you let him go?"

"Do you really think we would've been able to stop him?" Fane touched his cheek ruefully.

Tor had once caved it in with a single strike of his fist. Even though Fane was a full artilect, Tor was almost as strong as he was. And when he was in a rage…

"Besides, we were too busy trying to keep you alive. Tor's a hunter. He knows how to make himself

12

inconspicuous and disappear. He left while no one was watching."

"So you think he killed himself? That's not the kind of person he is."

"Ailith, *none* of us are the people we were," Oliver reminded me.

"What do you think I saw then?" *I know what I saw. Tor is alive.*

Cindra squeezed my shoulder, her expression uncertain. "Maybe your mind is playing tricks on you. You've been through a lot in the past few weeks—you're in a new body, for God's sake. And you're desperate to find him. Who knows how your mind is trying to help you cope? Or maybe the strain… A lot's happened. Callum, your father dying—"

"I know what I saw." Something occurred to me. "What if they captured him and did to him what they did to Ella? He said he couldn't feel his body, that he was in the dark. What if they've hidden his consciousness away?"

Ella, one of the cyborgs of our cluster, had discovered information our creators hadn't wanted her to know. To ensure their secret wouldn't be exposed, they'd let her body die and contained her consciousness in a tiny black box tucked away on a dusty shelf.

I turned to the one person who might be able to give me an answer. Pax. He stared at the spilled bait slowly disappearing among the among the jade-tinted waves.

"Pax?"

He finally looked at me. "There was only one future where he lived. Only one where he didn't—" He dropped his gaze.

Oliver cleared his throat loudly, and Pax, for once, took the hint.

I grabbed Pax's shoulders. Although he tended toward

thinness, the last few weeks had been kind to him, and he'd filled out with new strength. Still, it was nothing compared to my need for answers. "What future is that? Pax tell me. In the future where Tor survives, what happened to him?"

He scraped a gray-striped shell over some pebbles with the toe of his boot, his eyes on the ground.

"Pax?"

He looked at me and bit his lip. "The only way for Tor to survive is if the Cosmists have him."

He's been sneaking out to meet me. He has a good excuse. I mean, they have to eat, right? Mom and Dad wouldn't approve of a relationship between us. They'd say he's too old, too different. That he couldn't possibly be interested in me, not truly. But they don't know him like I do. All he wants is to have a normal life.

—Love, Grace

05
AILITH

"The *Cosmists* have him?" I repeated.

Pax nodded.

"But how—?" My vision telescoped as Eire's ability took over. *The past.*

The image was ghostly and insubstantial like the figures in my dream, but his identity was unmistakable. Tor stumbled over the rough ground of the forest, still covered in my blood. Unyielding branches scratched his face, blinding him, the skin on his knees and palms scraped away by the treacherous roots that brought him down over and over again. And still he pressed forward, sleeping where he collapsed, his mind freed by dehydration and grief.

Then, on the third night, his delirium inexplicably broke, and he turned back the way he'd come, his steps irregular with renewed urgency.

In his weakened state, he didn't sense her. *Kalbir.* She

crept up behind him, striking him on the back of the head and nearly knocking him out. Tor fought back, but with his blunted reflexes, she'd easily gained the upper hand. Before he could recover, she injected him in the neck, and for him, everything went dark.

"Ailith?" Cindra leaned over and peered into my face.

"Pax is right. Ethan has Tor. That traitorous bitch ambushed him." They didn't need to ask who I meant. Kalbir had not only betrayed and exposed us but murdered my father before joining Ethan's ranks. "We've got to rescue him."

Pebbles and mollusk husks crunched underfoot as a group of four non-augmented humans approached us. Among them was a family—Ryan, Lily, and Grace had lived in Goldnesse, the town where I'd grown up, and the town where we'd been exposed. Where my father had died. The town whose people Ethan had taken over. When he convinced the community to gather their pitchforks and turn on us, Lily and Ryan had risked everything to warn us. Since there was a good chance Ethan would've killed them if they'd returned after what he saw as their betrayal, they'd come with us, braving an uncertain future with their sixteen-year-old daughter Grace.

She hung back as they joined us. Lily had told Cindra and me in confidence that Grace was pining for her old life, although who or what specifically she wasn't sure. Lily still worried about those they'd left behind—she'd been one of the few nurses in the community—but both she and Ryan seemed to be adjusting well to life on the island, their faces ruddy with the sea air and their hands roughened by new work.

Stella, the fourth, had been one of Ethan's followers. Although she was a Cosmist and believed in the superiority of artificial intelligence in general and artilects in particular, she didn't believe cyborgs were an abomination like the rest of them. She too had risked Ethan's wrath to aid us, and although we knew her actions would've been different if Fane hadn't sided with us, we were grateful nonetheless.

"I think Tor's alive. Ethan has him." The shock on their faces mirrored the churning in my gut.

"What are you going to do?" Stella asked. She looked as nauseated as I felt. Even though our fight with Ethan was far from over, the relative peace of the past few weeks had given us a false sense of security.

"Nothing yet," Oliver said.

"But—"

"But nothing. Look, Ailith, I'm willing to give you the benefit of the doubt and accept that what you saw *could be* real and Tor *might be* alive, but we need to make *sure* what you're seeing is real before we go throwing ourselves in front of a Cosmist juggernaut. And if it is true, and the Cosmists do have Tor, we're going to have to come up with a damn good plan to get him back. If they've taken over the compound, it's not like we can just walk through the front door."

"We may not have time, Oliver. Why did he suddenly surface now, if they've had him all this time? They must have something planned, either for him or us. Look, I agree we need to be as sure as we can be." *I know he's alive.* "But we may have to come up with a plan on the way."

Oliver scrubbed his hands over his face. "I know. I know you're right. Plus, if they do have him, they may be able to use him against us. Sorry." He grimaced in apology.

"He would never—" I began. But— *Oliver is right. The Tor we know would never willingly hurt us, but we don't know what Ethan might do to him.*

Oliver held up a hand. "We knew they'd come for us. And if they've got Tor, our only advantage is that they don't know where we are right now, but how long will that last? They probably have scouts out looking for us at this very moment. We need to act first. If we can find out that Tor's still alive, and that they're still at the compound, maybe we can preempt their attack."

"What if they *want* us to come and get him?" I said slowly. "What if he's *bait*? He doesn't know I'm alive, but they do." The thought of his grief was more than I could bear.

Oliver closed his eyes and grimaced again. "That would make sense. Fuck. Okay. Even if that's true, I still think we should take the offensive and go after him. If we do it quickly enough, maybe we'll be able to surprise them."

"And how do you propose we do that? It's too risky, Oliver. I thought we were going to find ways to protect ourselves, *here*." Ryan's voice was strained, and I didn't blame him. They were caught in the middle of our fight and didn't have our millions of nanites to repair their injuries and keep them alive.

"Not *we*. You're not coming. You're right, we need to fortify ourselves here. That's going to be your job." Oliver gestured to the four of them. "Though, this plan may actually work out great for you—if they do manage to get us, they probably won't come for you. So, silver lining and all that."

Ryan didn't look convinced. "Why can't we just go somewhere else? Somewhere they can't find us?"

"I don't think such a place exists. Not where we can survive, anyway. They find a way, Ryan. Sooner or later, they'll track us down. Fane is too important to them."

"It's true," Fane admitted. "They need me to build more artilects. They were so concerned with secrecy, they kept very few records. And much of what they did have has been destroyed. However, if they get hold of this—"

He tapped his temple. "They'll have all the information they need." He gave me a grim smile. "I agree with Oliver—Ryan and the others should stay here and make some plans while the rest of us try to retrieve Tor. If he *is* alive, we'll need all the strength we can get."

"*You're* not coming, Fane. It's you they want." My tone was harsh, but hurting his feelings was better than the tendrils of panic that began to unfurl at the thought of the Cosmists capturing him.

"You can't stop me." His voice was calm, but the set of his jaw told me he was anything but.

"Fane—"

He gazed dreamily off into the distance, humming under his breath as he ignored me.

Fine. Maybe he *was* better off with us. If something did go wrong, at least we could try to protect him. No offense to Ryan and the others, but they were no match for Ethan.

"The first thing we need to do is find out whether what you saw is true. Do you think you could connect with him again?" Oliver asked.

"I can try, though I might not be able to get through if he's unconscious again. But I *know* he's alive—his thread would be dark otherwise."

Oliver looked dubious.

"If Tor's unconscious, do you think you could connect with Kalbir?" Cindra asked tentatively. She knew my feelings all too well.

Oliver dismissed the idea with a wave of his hand. "If Ethan's as knowledgeable about us as I think he is, he'll have found some way to block you from going down her thread. He might not tell Kalbir everything, but she's bound to have some knowledge of his and Lien's plans. He wouldn't want to risk us finding out."

"It's still worth an attempt, though, isn't it?" Cindra

asked.

I glanced at Oliver. "Could it hurt? Is there any way they'd be able to track us through her?"

He deliberated for a moment then shook his head. "No. Not that I know of. Be careful, though, in case he's rigged her with some kind of virus. Get out at the first sign of anything unusual."

"I will." I closed my eyes and the network of threads spread out before me. Kalbir's thread was invisible. Not dark—simply not there. "I think Oliver's right. I can't find Kalbir's thread."

"So Tor's our only option then." Oliver sounded relieved.

"It seems so, unless we want to go in blind. But I have a feeling Ethan *wants* us to find Tor—he'd have blocked his thread otherwise." *In which case, this should be easy.*

In the darkness, Tor's thread flickered. Its gleam was muted, but even as I watched, it seemed to grow brighter. As though *he* were growing stronger. Our instincts were right—something was about to happen.

I kissed him today. He was hesitant, dreading her reaction. They have a very close bond, and even though things haven't always been easy between them, at the moment they were in a good place, and he didn't want to ruin that. So I lied and said it was my birthday, even though it had passed weeks ago. When I told him, he leaned over and kissed me. I pretended to stumble so that I could press my lips hard against his. He was surprised at first, but then he put his arms around me. The silver rain could come tomorrow, and I wouldn't care.

—Love, Grace

06

TOR

The line of light expanded as a door opened, framing the silhouette of a shapely pair of calves. The brightness was too much for my eyes, and I shrank back. We both waited for the other to speak.

She gave in first. Patience was never really her strong suit.

"Hello, Tor."

"Kalbir. Where am I? What did you do to me?"

"You're at the compound. I dragged your sorry ass back here."

"How did you find me?"

"It wasn't that difficult." She snorted. "Crashing around in the woods like a drunk bear. A child could've found you."

She waited in vain for me to respond.

"God, you're pathetic, Tor. I knew you'd come back for the others— you're so predictable," she taunted me.

21

I stayed silent.

She threw her hands in the air. "Well, if you're not going to talk—"

"Let me go, Kalbir. What am I even doing here?"

"That isn't an option. Ethan has plans for you."

"So you're Ethan's pet now, is that it?"

For some reason, that rankled her. "I'm not his pet. It's more than that." But there was doubt in her voice and her smile was too quick. "Why? Are you jealous?"

"Hardly. How long have I been here?"

"Six weeks."

"Six weeks? But I—" It couldn't have been six weeks. I had no idea how much time had passed, but surely it couldn't have been that long?

"You've been unconscious, Tor. Ethan wanted to keep you quiet until he was ready."

"Ready for what?" I was pretty sure I already knew the answer.

"You know what. You're going to be the one to help retrieve him."

"Him?"

"Don't play dumb, Tor. It doesn't suit you. You know damn well I mean Fane. Ethan wants him back."

"I'll never help you find him. Or them."

"We're not interested in them. And as for Fane, we don't need you to find him."

"What exactly do you need me for then?"

"You're the muscle, obviously. We both know he won't come willingly." She gave a humorless chuckle.

"Why can't you do it?" We both had enhanced physical strength. Even though her build was smaller than mine, in terms of physical power, she rivaled me.

She looked away. "I let Ethan dampen my ability. He wanted proof that I wasn't secretly plotting against him."

"You did what? Kalbir, how could you let him do that?" Even though I could never forgive Kalbir for the things she'd done, she was *still one of us.*

"Don't you dare judge me, Tor. I trust him. And if this is what he needs to trust me, I'll do it."

"You're a fool, Kalbir. He's going to destroy you. And us. Why would I help you?"

She ignored the first part of my comment. "If you don't, we'll kill you," she said simply.

"I don't care if you kill me, Kalbir. I've already lost what mattered most to me. Surely you realize that by now?"

She hesitated and looked as if she were about to say something. Whatever it was, she held back. "We'll kill them. *You remember them, the cyborgs you abandoned? You know, she would've hated how weak you are. How weak she made you. She would've despised you."*

I didn't have to ask who she meant. I also knew she was right. "She's dead." So I would despise myself enough for both of us.

"Yes, she is. And the others will be too if you refuse to help us."

"What happened to you, Kalbir?"

"The same things that happened to you, only I want to live." She dropped a container onto the floor in front of my face. "Eat up. You'll need your strength."

07

AILITH

"Pax is right. Tor's alive, but he's with Ethan and the other Cosmists, including Kalbir."

"Shit." Oliver put his head into his hands. He hastily added, "No, I'm glad, but we're going to have to go rescue them, aren't we?"

"Tor, yes. Kalbir, no. She's officially with Ethan. She's even allowed him to put a muzzle on her ability."

Cindra looked as disgusted as I felt. "Why would she *do* that? I mean, how could she? After everything he's done."

"I got the impression she's in love with him," I said.

Cindra's mouth hardened into a grim line. "Then she's a fool."

"That's what Tor told her," I replied. "Look, I'm going after him. I don't expect the rest of you—"

"Don't be ridiculous." Oliver put one hand over his forehead and fluttered his eyelashes. "My name is Ailith, and I'm going to be martyred as a saint when I grow up."

"That doesn't even make sense," I said. "You can't—"

"So your decision is made then," Ryan interrupted. "I guess there's no use trying to talk you out of it, is there?"

"No. If we stay here, Ethan will come for us. Retrieving Tor will give us our best chance at defending ourselves. And like Oliver said before—if something does happen to us, they won't come looking for you. And if we *do* make it back here with Tor… Either way, your family is as protected as they can be." My rationale wasn't as altruistic as it seemed; the last thing we needed to worry about was protecting them on the road. "Unless you think you might be safer going away on your own?"

The stricken look on Ryan's face gave me his answer.

"This is between Ethan and us," I continued. "And I'm sorry you got caught in the middle. I promise we'll—" *No. Don't make promises you can't keep. They've been through enough.* "We'll do everything we can to keep us all safe. We're even going to try to find allies on the way. But, Ryan," I lowered my voice, "if we're not back within ten days, you'll need to stop waiting and do what you think is best for Grace and Lily."

"I understand." He seemed exhausted.

I looked back at the others. "Let's get ready. We leave first thing in the morning."

As they hurried away, Fane opened his mouth to speak.

"Don't even think about volunteering to sacrifice yourself, Fane."

"I wasn't—I want to live. I just… Tor might be different. He thinks you're dead." He frowned, marring his perfect skin. "Do you think Kalbir knows you're not?"

The memory of her words to him stung. "If she does,

she didn't say. But it doesn't matter. He'll find out soon enough. After that…well, we'll deal with the rest."

Fane didn't look convinced. "Things between the two of you might be different. If he thought he'd lost you forever then realizes he hasn't…it may change his perspective on the two of you."

"Fane, are you worried? About…us?"

"Do you mean jealous? No, but—"

"You have nothing to worry about." I stood on my tiptoes and kissed him. I still wasn't sure what my relationship with Fane was. Shortly after we met, Tor and I began a romantic relationship, but my ability to control him and my refusal to give it up had caused tension between us. Tor had cut the physical side of our relationship short, but of course, those feelings remained, and given our unique bond, probably always would. We just couldn't see a way to make it work.

With Fane, it was…easier. Our history was less complicated. But under his gorgeous exterior, he was a machine. A fully-sentient, self-aware intelligence, but still…not only was he not human, he wasn't even technically alive. Most of the time I forgot, but when I did remember, it gave me pause. Did it *matter* that he wasn't human? My gut instinct was that no, it didn't. His feelings for me *weren't* a program, like Tor had feared our attraction was. But even if they were, the result was the same.

Red petals on bare skin. Something sticky, something sweet.

I let myself relax into the images, Fane's artilect equivalent of emotions. Created from millions of data, the impressions gave me a quantifiable, near-human approximation of his feelings. He might not have been sure of my feelings, but I was always aware of his, and it was one of the things that made a relationship with him simpler.

I pulled back. *Stop. This isn't the time. Wait until we've got Tor back and you've got the luxury to worry about something like romance.*

It seemed like Fane *could* tell what I was thinking after all. "Now's not a good time, is it?" he asked, smiling ruefully.

My confusion evaporated as I laughed. Whatever happened in the future, we were here now, and I knew all too well how temporary that could be. I linked my hands behind his neck and pulled his face down to mine. "Fane, you're *always* a good time."

***

The next morning, as we stood packed and ready to leave, Ryan, Lily, and Stella huddled together in the brisk early-morning air to wave us off. Lily's eyes were rimmed with red and Stella's were sunken above dark shadows. Ryan was outwardly stoic, but the tense set of his shoulders told me otherwise. I couldn't say I blamed them. We were leaving them, and they knew there was no guarantee we would return, despite our best intentions. Surely after what I'd told Ryan, they'd developed a contingency plan— several, if I knew Lily as well as I thought I did. But still. Their chances of survival were better when we were together.

Unless, of course, you considered the danger we would bring to their door if we succeeded. No matter how I looked at it, in trying to keep us all safe, we were about to make life much more difficult for them.

"I don't think we'll be able to stay in contact with you for more than a day or two. We'll be too far away for radio by the time we reach the compound." I tried to think of something more positive to say but came up empty.

27

"We'll be fine," Lily said, her voice more confident than her face. "Ailith, if Mil and Lexa are alive—"

Lily had been close to our creators, back when she'd thought they were ordinary scientists who'd survived the apocalypse in their underground lab. When she'd discovered the truth—that they'd not only harbored the cyborgs they'd created but had also been responsible for the silver rain that had killed millions of people in the aftermath of the war—she'd been devastated. It was one of the reasons they'd chosen to leave with us, rather than stay in the relative safety of the compound. Was Lily regretting that decision now? Did living with the people who'd intended to cyberize people against their will seem preferable to taking their chances with us?

"How can you feel for them? After everything they did?" Cindra yanked at the straps on her pack with more force than needed. She'd also been close to Lexa, and the betrayal had cut deep.

Ryan put his arm around Lily's shoulders. "She feels for everyone, you know that." It was true. Lily was one of those people who tried to see the good in everyone and give them the benefit of the doubt. Including us. *And look where that got her.*

"What they did was unforgivable. But the people I knew them as were…different, good. They really were trying to help us build a future. They could still do that here. It would be a second chance for them."

It would actually be a third or fourth chance, but I wasn't going to argue. "I won't make any promises."

Lily nodded, understanding that that was the best she was going to get.

"Where's Grace? Is she angry that we're leaving?"

Grace had seemed agitated yesterday after we'd announced our plans. She'd gone to bed early, which wasn't unusual for her. She'd been temperamental ever since we'd left the Okanagan. Some days she seemed fine and was chatty and interested, asking Cindra to show her how to make various things, or sitting with Fane and quizzing him about being an artilect. Other days she retreated from us, staying withdraw and sullen in her room.

"She's upset. She still can't accept that so many people turned on us. She had to leave her friends, her school. And now with you going away… It's too many changes, too fast."

"Well, give her our love when you do see her. Tell her it'll be fine, that we'll be back."

Lily crossed her arms over her chest. "I'll tell her that you'll try your best. I'm tired of making promises to her then letting her down," she said, echoing my earlier thoughts. "When she was a child, it was different. She forgave so easily then."

Fane tried to hide his feelings from me as I followed him down to the beach, but he couldn't stop his apprehension from flashing through my mind.

The scent of burnt coffee. A hedge maze with a single exit. A bird plummeting into the ocean.

08

AILITH

As we passed the skeletons of the old olive trees, Pax
tucked something under a large rock at the base of one of
the trunks. He'd discovered little caches all over the
island—notes that people had written and trinkets they'd
left, which he gave to Cindra for her growing archive of
our history. He'd taken to leaving his own notes and
charms all over the island, although when I'd asked him
who would ever find them, he'd just shrugged and smiled
his enigmatic smile. I was desperate to take it as a good sign
that someone might be there in the future, so I didn't ask
anything else.

The boat we'd come over to the island in rocked gently
against the beach. What would I have done if I'd had a boat

when the war started? Would I have jumped in and sailed away, hoping to find safety over the water? Or would I have gone home, braving a firestorm for fear of an even greater unknown?

When we'd reached the coast weeks ago, we'd avoided the major harbor close to Vancouver, one of the first cities to be destroyed in the bombing. Instead, we'd ventured farther south, and it had worked in our favor. In a tiny abandoned coastal resort, we'd found a boat large enough for all of us and our supplies. Best of all, it was hydrogen-powered, gathering its energy from the saltwater itself.

"I wonder what happened to the owners?" Pax had asked. As he did, I saw them, pale specters glancing back over their shoulders as they abandoned their craft. They'd walked into one of the resort villas close by and never left.

I'd kept the information to myself.

Now, as Oliver steered us away from the beach we'd come to call home, I lay on the deck next to Fane and let the briny sea air scour my skin.

"Do you think we'll find any allies on the mainland?" I asked him. When I'd said it to Ryan, it hadn't seemed that unreasonable. But thinking about it now… "I don't want to rely too much on the idea, but—"

"I know you are alive."

"Umbra?" *Shit.* When we'd been unable to find Callum's body, we'd figured she'd probably survived in some form, but we'd hoped fervently that we were wrong.

Fane looked at me sharply.

"They told me everything. How he brought your body back. How they fixed you."

"You're alive? Is Callum?"

Fane gestured to Pax and Cindra to come closer. Oliver must've seen them gathering through the window because he put the boat on an automatic course.

"Yes. And no. He was too fragile."

"You killed him, you mean."

"Yes."

And suddenly, I saw Callum. Or more accurately, I saw *through* him. He lay on the ground next to my body, horrified as my blood soaked into the dusty earth. A cactus had gotten tangled in my hair, and he wanted desperately to pull it out.

"I'm sorry," he wanted to say. He opened his mouth, but only Umbra was there.

Then Tor was upon us, his disbelieving hands trying to put the remains of my skull back together. Watching, I wanted to scream at him to go, to look away, but the time for that had passed weeks ago.

Sobbing, he did the best he could, tying his jacket around my head, leaving only what was left of my face exposed. He gathered me into his arms, cradling my ruined face against his shoulder, then turned and spat on Callum, blinding him. "I'll be back for you, Umbra, I promise you that." He grew smaller and smaller as he lurched away, hoping beyond hope that I could be saved.

Callum lay in the dust, wishing he'd died too, when approaching footsteps shook the ground under his head. A thrill of Umbra's delight swept through him.

"The Saints are here. They have found us."

"This won't turn out the way you think it will, Umbra. I'll never survive long enough for them to do anything with you." Callum tried to hold his breath, his last defense against her.

"Breathe," she demanded and touched a nerve. Searing pain darted through Callum's spine, and he gasped, taking a deep breath.

"They will keep you alive, Callum. As long as it takes. I am their god. The one they have been waiting for."

And they did. For twenty-eight excruciating hours,

Callum had lived as the nanites and the Saints fought to keep him breathing until they could find a way to make Umbra flesh. But finally, at the turn of the twenty-ninth hour, Callum won. His heart came to his aid and simply refused to beat any longer. He died with a smile on his lips. He'd finally beaten her, the being he'd once loved so much.

Or so he'd thought. *I'm glad he'd died believing it.* Now, we just had to make sure it came true.

"How are we communicating? You never had that kind of power."

"It does not matter. I want my body."

"Your body?"

"Yes. You took my body."

"We gave you the chance to have this body, Umbra, and you turned it down. It's not yours anymore."

"It is mine. You promised."

"If we're talking, you must've been fixed. You must've been given a body."

"I was."

"So what's the problem?"

"My new body does not…feel."

"What do you mean?"

"I cannot feel. Or taste. It is too primitive."

"You became used to Callum's humanity, and now you can't live without it? How galling for you."

"Yes."

"Well, what a shame you killed him then."

"I want my body."

"It's not your body, Umbra."

There was silence. And then, *"It will be."* And she was gone.

Imagine our surprise when we received a radio transmission from Umbra. It seems our steadfast devotion in the face of false idols has paid off. And she needs our help. The Cyborgists tried to stop us from joining with our Messiah by encasing her in the body of one of their own in a gross mockery of her divinity. But she need not fear. We will find her and release her from her flesh cocoon, allowing her metamorphosis into Divinity.

—Celeste Steed, The Second Coming

09

AILITH

I opened my eyes to the others' concerned faces.

"Ailith, what's going on?" Cindra asked.

"Umbra's alive. She just spoke to me." I closed my eyes and pressed my fingertips against the lids. *Just what we need.*

"And Callum?"

"Callum's dead." We'd all assumed, but *knowing* still hit hard. Although none of us had had enough time to really get to know him, through our connection, I'd been privy to some of the most intense moments of his life. Grief and something darker sprouted inside me; before this was over, I would have my reckoning with Umbra.

Oliver, ever practical, was incredulous. "How are you talking to Umbra? It shouldn't be possible."

"She's been…fixed up. I have no idea by whom."

"I do," Fane said. "It means she's also with Ethan. From what Oliver told me, The Saints of Loving Grace don't have the knowledge or equipment to give her a functional body. If the Saints *did* manage to retrieve Callum's body as they'd planned, Umbra could easily have told them about Ethan and his resources. I can't see him or Lien turning down a chance to resurrect even a primitive AI."

The thought of Ethan and the Saints teaming up was chilling.

"Even so, how's it possible that she's speaking to me?"

Oliver looked at me as though I were an idiot. "Ethan's has access to Lexa and Mil's equipment. Plus, don't forget we all came from the same original designs. They likely combined some of Pax's programming and some of Fane's."

"You can't be serious," Cindra said. "Why would they have given her *any* power?"

Fane was thoughtful. "If Ethan's given her special abilities, it must be that they suit an ulterior motive."

"So what does that mean for us? How could he use her against us?"

"To beat Fane, perhaps? What better way to fight an artilect than with an artilect? They know he's not going to come quietly."

"She couldn't beat you, Fane, could she?" Cindra asked.

"I don't know," he replied. "Before all of this, I would've said no. But who knows what they've done to her?" He turned, his expression uneasy. "Pax? Can she beat me?"

"Yes."

"*Does* she beat me?" Fane asked, looking alarmed.

Pax pulled at a loose thread on his sweater then smiled at Fane. "Sometimes."

"Okay, stop. It won't help to worry about this right now." If my nerves stretched any tighter, I would explode. *Could she really defeat Fane? Take my body?* I was very aware that although it was mine now, it hadn't always been.

"You think she's coming for us? God, I need a drink." Oliver hung over the railing as though he were contemplating leaping.

The salty air on my skin was suddenly irritating. I wrapped a blanket around my shoulders. "She might. I don't know how much agency she has. She may not be able to go anywhere without Ethan's will, but she'd never let us know that. Or she might wait and let Ethan do the heavy lifting. I mean, we *are* heading right for them. Maybe she'll just bide her time."

"You'd think she'd have kept quiet then, not let you know she was alive and after your body," Cindra mused.

"Maybe she's more human than you give her credit for. She was built by one, after all," Fane said. "Maybe she just can't resist."

"I don't know if Umbra having human shortcomings makes me feel better or worse," I remarked.

The troubled look Fane gave me made it clear.

Worse. Because impatience might be one of them.

***

We moored the boat in a small, hidden cove then rowed the rest of the way to the tawny sand beach. Before the War, it must've been a popular tourist spot—secluded, with just the right amount of adjacent wilderness to give the illusion of a private island.

If I concentrated, Eire's ability likely would've shown me. But it would've shown me other things as well. Couples watching the sun go down for the last time before wading out to sea, reassuring their children that all would be well if only they didn't hold their breath—too many things I couldn't unsee. I'd thought my ability to see into the minds of other was a curse, but it was nothing compared to Eire's visions of the past.

How did you stand it?

I never left the room I was in, Ailith. The only ghost there was me. Fragments of both Eire and Ella had stayed with me, whispering to me and to each other. The continuing love between them, a love that was almost tangible to me, was the only thing that made having Eire's ability bearable.

We walked a few hundred yards into the camouflaging forest, a habit Tor had taught us, and dropped our gear into a pile.

"Right," Oliver said, pulling a map out of his pack and shaking it open. "Let's figure out a route then start walking. We should be able to get— Oh, for fuck's sake!" he burst out as the map refused to open, tearing instead and leaving him with nothing but a scrap between his fingers.

"Here, let me help you." Cindra stifled a laugh and bent to retrieve the unruly chart.

"Are you still thinking about Umbra?" Fane asked, startling me. He moved even more silently than we did.

"Well, now I am," I replied. "I was thinking of Eire."

"If Umbra does come after us—"

As though on cue, a rustling shook the scrubby undergrowth behind us.

We all dropped into a crouch and froze, scanning the spaces between the wasted trees. Fane held a finger to his lips and crept noiselessly toward the sound. The rest of us tried to melt into the background—another of Tor's lessons. Fane disappeared from sight, and we heard a slight scuffle before he emerged holding the arm of a very bedraggled Grace.

"Looks like we had a stowaway," he said as she glared up at him.

Since we'd taken the only rowboat, she'd had to swim to shore. Her hair hung in dripping ropes, and she shivered despite her defiance.

"Grace! What are you doing here?" Cindra had already untied a blanket from her pack and was shaking it open.

"I want…wanted to help," she said as she begrudgingly accepted the blanket. "Thanks."

I stepped away. The chattering of her teeth dredged up some disturbing memories of Nova's teeth chipping and cracking against each other as she bit at the stale air of the bunker. I closed my eyes. *Breathe. Slowly.*

"Grace, you can't come with us," Cindra said, her voice kind but firm. "Your parents are going to be worried sick. They must've discovered you're missing by now."

"I'm a grown woman." A deep blush spread across her cheeks.

"Grace, it's not about that. It's about it being dangerous. You must know that. Our abilities protect us."

"I… I thought if I helped you, you would turn me into one of you. Then I would have abilities, and I could—"

"Oh, Grace. We can't. And even if we could, it's too dangerous. You've seen what our life is like. You have to go home." Cindra's tone was low and reassuring, but Grace collapsed as though Cindra had struck her.

She began to cry. Cindra knelt and hugged her thin shoulders while Oliver and Pax stood awkwardly to the side, unsure of where to look.

"Why do you want to be a cyborg?" I asked, as gently as I could.

"Do you have any idea what it's like? How *small* I feel? I'm scared to live in this world and not be special. It means I won't survive. I'm too small," she repeated brokenly.

"Grace, I'm so, so sorry," I said as she clung to Cindra and sobbed.

"So what are we going to do now?" Oliver asked. "We can't take her with us, and we can't leave her here. We'll have to turn back." I hoped Grace didn't see the annoyance on his face.

"Or she could come with us. She *should* come." Pax was looking at Grace with a new interest. One I didn't like.

"Pax, did you know she was going to come?" I asked him. *Damn it, Pax.*

"It was a possibility."

"And you didn't tell us because you knew we would stop her?" I asked, even though I knew the answer.

He nodded solemnly.

"I thought you didn't want to keep getting involved. Ryan and Lily are—"

"I promise I'll do what you say," Grace interrupted, her eyes suddenly dry.

Hmmm. "Why do you *really* want to come with us, Grace? If you know that we can't make you a cyborg and that you're going to spend days hiking directly into danger, why do you still want to come?"

I could almost see her mind working as she tried to come up with a more convincing story. My own parents must've seen that look on my face many times.

"Grace?" I imitated my mother, using her best no-nonsense voice.

Her shoulders slumped as she gave up. "I need to see him," she whispered.

"Him?" For a moment, I was confused. "Do you mean Tor?"

She started to shake her head as though to deny it then gave up. "Yes." A rosy blush bloomed on her cheeks, and she kept her eyes on the ground.

Oh my god, does she have a crush on Tor? Is she in love with him? For her to be willing to risk her life for him, she must be. Not for the first time, I wished I could talk to the others with my mind, rather than just seeing through them. *What do we do now?* I glanced at Cindra, who shook her head.

If Pax believes she's important…

"Okay, fine, Grace. You can come. But you have to do exactly what we tell you, and—"

"I will!" She shot to her feet. "You won't regret it, I swear. I love him—" She gasped for breath as another sob shook her.

Did I have that much passion at sixteen?

I looked at Cindra again, and this time, she shrugged. Over her shoulder, Pax nodded.

Grace smiled through her tears, rubbing her sleeve over her face. "I promise I'll help you. I won't be a burden."

I didn't like it. If Pax thought she needed to come, it meant she was going to play a role, and yet again, we might sacrifice someone for our cause. Because the truth was, in terms of the bigger picture, she *was* expendable, just like she'd feared. *Poor Ryan and Lily.* What would they do when they discovered her missing?

"We'd better go back to the boat and radio your parents, Grace. The last thing they need right now is even more worry." I started walking back the way we'd come. "It won't take long."

"No," said Grace quickly. "You can't."

"Don't worry. I promise you can come with us. I just want them to know you're all right."

"It's not that," she said, her face darkening from rose to crimson. "I trashed the radio. Just in case you didn't let me come with you, I didn't want you to be able to call them." She crossed her arms over her chest.

"For fuck's sake, Grace, do you have any idea—"

Oliver's harsh tone made her flinch.

"I'm sorry, I just—" Tears shone in her eyes again.

"We have to get going." Cindra was looking at the sky. "We need to get at least part of the way before we camp for the night.

Cindra was right. Whatever had happened, we couldn't worry about it now.

Pax pointed to a place on Oliver's torn map. "Here," he said, his finger landing on a spot that looked just like a million others. "We need to be *right here.*"

Hi. My name is Pax. I don't know if anyone will ever find this, since I don't know what our ultimate timeline will be, BUT, if everything goes the way it should, you will find this, so I've tried to make it as weatherproof as possible. I hope things haven't been too difficult for you. I did my best, but things didn't always turn out the way we planned.

10

WILLIAM

Day: 2000 A.W.

"*For those of you folks who are just joining us, the A.W. stands for both Artilect War and After War. Clever, really.*"

I rapped my knuckles on smooth, cold metal. The resulting ding was disappointing—more of a donk and not at all the resonating flourish I'd hoped for. It didn't penetrate the darkness further than my own hand.

It was still just Lars and me. Good old Lars. Every day he went a little madder. I guess he hadn't made provisions for that part of his plan. Oh, Lars, you mad, mad bastard. But maybe I was mad too.

"Or maybe, and this is a big maybe, folks, Lars is the sane one here and I'm the one whose mind has gone." It was possible.

"I wish you all would stop playing dead—unless you really are dead." Sometimes I wished I was. But God, who knew what Lars would do to me then? If I were lucky, he wouldn't even notice.

"But I'm not dead. Not yet, anyway. Just stuck here with Lars *and the rest of you in this oubliette. How do I know that word? Oubliette?" I tapped again on the metal casing. "It doesn't matter. Soon, I'll play dead too. And before long, I actually will be." I grinned into the dark.*

"And then you, fine folks, you and Lars will have to find other entertainment." The silence made me reconsider.

"Although, my death might be the only entertainment you need. You can talk about it amongst yourselves for years to come. The final curtain."

Should today be the day? How should I take my bow?

"Shall we have a vote?" I took their silence as assent. "Slit my wrists?" No. Knowing my luck, I'd do it wrong, and just a get a nasty infection. Then Lars would have to take care of me. And from what I'd heard of him mumbling to himself, I definitely didn't want his ministrations.

Although, the delirium of infection might be a nice vacation for me.

"Starvation?" I didn't think that would be possible. Too many supplies here. And again, Lars. He knew how to keep people alive on very little.

Plus, who was I kidding? I knew I could never starve; I was rather short on willpower.

"Will Power. Ha! Get it? Maybe I should change my last name. We'll vote on that one later." I felt through the blackness, my fingers coming to rest on snaking coils of cable.

"Electrocution? Now we're talking. Of course, that would leave you all in the lurch, wouldn't it? Though it might wake a few of you up."

I waited for a reply, just in case. Nothing.

"Maybe we'll just put this vote to the side for a day or two. No need to be hasty, right?"

Not a single dissenting voice.

"I'm glad we all agree. That's why I like you guys so much." Strains of orchestral music and the low hum of voices filtered through

the gloom.

"That's enough chitchat. I can hear the band striking up. It looks like it's time for another party. Well, God knows we've got a lot to celebrate." I felt my way to the door then turned back.

"I've got work to do. Shall we meet tomorrow? Same time, same place?" I cupped my hand over my ear.

"What? Of course, I'll still be here. Oubliette, remember?"

No way out.

II

AILITH

I started awake with a gasp, the cyborg's words ringing in my head. His voice had been strange, almost muffled.

Who is William? Something nagged at the back of my mind. William. Maybe Pax would know. After all, he'd been the one who'd insisted on camping here. Did he know something was going to happen? If so, why hadn't he told me?

"Pax? Are you awake?" Nothing. *"Pax!"* Nope. He slept like the dead. Whatever the mystery was, it would have to

wait until morning.

"Fuck," I said to no one in particular.

"Ailith?" Fane ducked his head through the tent flap. Since he didn't need to sleep the way we did, he'd been standing guard. "What's wrong?"

"I think there's another cyborg here, one who's been here since the war. He called himself William. I think Pax knew about him, and that's why he wanted us to camp here." *Now, why is the name William so familiar? Come on, Ailith, think.*

It hit me. William. Nova. William was the cyborg who was supposed to have been in the bunker with Oliver. "William was one of the cyborgs in our generation. We'd thought he was dead. Why would he be out here, of all places? And he referred to a man named Lars and some others."

"Others? Cyborgs?" Fane slipped into the tent and sat next to me on top of the covers.

Something else was bothering me. Lars. *Lars. Oh my god.* "It can't be," I said. And yet, the coincidence was too great.

"It can't be what?" Fane asked. "Other cyborgs?"

"No, Lars."

"I don't follow."

"Nova. Before Oliver killed Nova, I saw her past. She worked as a caregiver for CIVRS addicts."

"The virtual reality system addicts? She was a caregiver?"

"Yes and no. They did…other things to them as well." I shook my head at his raised eyebrows. "You don't want to know. But she was there, just before she became a cyborg, delivering a baby. The doctor's name was Lars. But I don't think he was a real doctor." I thought back. *The front door opened; Lars had arrived. We nodded to each other. "Nurse."* *He knew damn well I wasn't a nurse, no more than he was a doctor.*

He worked for the government, same as me.

"Could he be the reason Nova was in the bunker with Oliver instead of William? She didn't seem to know it was going to happen, either of the times I was inside her."

They told me I was going to change the course of the world, that I had an extraordinary purpose. I would be the savior of the human race. I wouldn't end up like my wards, forgotten, degraded. No, I would be remembered forever.

And then, when she'd woken up: *I wasn't supposed to be here, in this shitty bunker. I should've been with them, carrying out my mission. Buying my freedom. Not trapped here, underground with him.*

"Whatever this Lars's involvement, I don't think Nova knew about it."

"And there are definitely others there? Do you think they could be the others involved in the switch? From what Oliver was telling me about Pantheon Modern security, it would have to have taken more than one person." He ran his hand down my spine.

"I don't know. It was a bit strange. He said it was just him and Lars, but then he spoke to the others. Only, no one answered."

Fane frowned. "He must've been speaking to himself."

"Maybe. But then he said they were having a party, and I heard voices." *Could there be others like us? Alive?*

"So other people, but not cyborgs?"

"No. I'd be able to tell if there were. Besides, Lexa and Mil said we were the only cyborgs of our generation who survived." Fane raised an eyebrow at me. "Yes, I know they've lied before, but why lie about that? Maybe it's doomsday preppers or something. But why would William be with them?"

"If he's a cyborg, why haven't you heard him before?"

It was a good question. William was close. So why *hadn't*

I heard him before? His thread was there—subdued, but present. "The connection felt a bit strange. A bit muted. Almost like—" Then it hit me. "Fane, I think he's underground. But there must be something else to it, because I could still link to the others when *they* were underground." I slipped out of the covers and put on my boots. "We've got to find him. If he's been trapped down there against his will all this time, he may be the ally we're looking for. Even if he isn't, he's one of us. Hurry, let's go wake the others."

"Wait until morning. It's the middle of the night, Ailith," he reminded me. "Everyone needs the rest. Besides, we should wait for what little light we can get. Stumbling around in the dark isn't going to make finding them any easier, *especially* if they aren't friendly."

He was right, but still. "I can't sleep, Fane." I had too many questions. Was William okay? He'd seemed a little…eccentric. Had they done something to him? Or was it just a side effect of being trapped underground all this time? How did he get there? And who were the others with him? My head threatened to explode.

"Well, I *don't* sleep. So why don't we distract each other?"

"You're supposed to be on guard."

"I'll keep my head outside the tent door."

"Fane—"

The brush of a butterfly's wings against a trumpet of foxglove.

He ran his strong hands over my bare back. *When did I take my shirt off?* I closed my eyes, glorying in the sensation. Although his skin felt like human skin, the palms of his hands and his fingers were completely smooth. They slid over me while images poured from him.

Sweet seeds of anise scattered on white linen.

I pressed into him, guiding him over onto his back and

pinning his arms over his head. He grinned; this was his favorite position because it had been his first. The first time we'd ever actually slept together, the first time he'd ever slept with anyone. Even now, a hint of the same wonder crept over his face, and his lips parted in a very human gasp.

He'd been built to resemble a man in every way, from his physique to the sensations he felt.

The perfect symmetry of a dahlia.

I straddled him, and he arched his hips as I guided him in, knotting his fists in the blanket behind his head.

The sharp scent of ginger, the bite of nutmeg.

His self-control lasted for only a few more seconds then he grabbed my hips and rocked into me as he sat up, wrapping his arms around me, pressing one hand into my lower back as though he could bring us even closer, gripping the back of my neck with the other. I moved my hips against his, and he threw his head back with an unselfconscious cry.

A trailing bouquet, held in trembling hands.

Jen,

I hope to God you find this. I waited for you as long as I could, but I can't wait any longer. Things are getting crazy here. I'm going to take the boat over to Dione Island, even though it's also gone dark. Please, if you find this, meet me there. I'll wait for you. And whatever you do, STAY OUT OF THE RAIN.

Shel.

12

AILITH

Even with our distraction, Fane and I were sitting around the campfire when the others emerged bleary-eyed and rubbing their hands together.

Oliver could tell immediately that something had happened. "All right, out with it, A. You're practically vibrating. What happened? What great evil do we face now?"

"Is it William?" Pax asked.

"Yes. You *knew* we'd meet William?"

"Not exactly. It was one of the possible paths, it just wasn't a very likely one. This is interesting. This is opening up futures I haven't seen before." Pax's expression softened, taking on a dreamy quality.

"Wait. Do you mean *our* William? The one Nova

replaced?" Oliver put the pieces together much quicker than I had.

"Yes. I think so," I said. "But—"

"Then where is he?" Oliver asked, looking around as though he expected William to be hiding in the bushes.

"Somewhere around here. I *think* he's underground. He… His communication was sort of muffled. But he's close. We just have to find him."

"Are we sure we want to? Do we need to risk any more enemies at this point? I mean, we don't know what his involvement with big switcheroo was."

I couldn't blame Oliver for that. We certainly had a habit of making enemies everywhere we went.

"No, but we need allies," Cindra said. "If he's a cyborg like us *and* one of our generation, this could be a good thing."

"Kalbir was also one of us," Oliver reminded her. "Maybe he was complicit. Or maybe he's a lunatic? What if that's why he's down there? Maybe something went wrong with his cyberization."

Given William's thoughts when I was inside him, that was a distinct possibility. Or, if he wasn't disturbed before, living underground in a bunker for five years may have taken its toll. But he'd said he wasn't alone.

Fane cleared his throat and gave me an expectant look.

Oliver crossed his arms over his chest. "What are you not telling us?"

I kept my expression bland. "I'm not sure what you mean." Oliver would never agree to go looking for William if he thought there were others.

"Fane is an artilect," Oliver pointed out. "His throat doesn't get dry."

I glared at Fane. *Judas.* "Fine. There might be other people down there with William."

Oliver was incredulous. "*What?* And you want to jeopardize us and Tor by bursting in on a bunch of—well, we don't even know what they are." He shook his head vehemently. "No. No way."

"Oliver—" I began.

"We can't leave him." Pax had drawn himself up to his full height, making him nearly six inches taller than Oliver. "If we can find William…we *need* to find William."

"See," I said to Oliver. "If Pax says—"

"*If Pax says,*" Oliver mimicked me. "We can't put ourselves into danger just because *Pax says.* How many times are we going to do this?"

"Until we end this. Look, I trust Pax. If he says we need William, I believe him. I don't think William chose to be there. I think he needs our help." I glanced around, entreating the others for support. "And like Cindra said, he might be the ally we need."

"He will be," Pax replied.

"See," I said to Oliver. "Pax—"

"Pax says." Oliver threw his hands in the air. "Unbelievable. You can't help yourself, can you? Did your parents never teach you about the consequences of sticking your nose in where it doesn't belong?"

"Oliver," I pleaded, "I think this is important. I need you to trust me."

"Ailith, it's not you I don't trust. But we need to pick our battles." He sighed and uncrossed his arms. "I know for a fact that we're going to regret this." He looked at Pax. "Right?"

Pax beamed at him. "A little bit."

Oliver covered his face with his hands and swore softly to himself.

Fane patted him on the back then turned to me. "Is there any chance this could be a trick?"

"I can't say for sure. But I don't think so. Look, I know Oliver might be right and we should just keep going and pretend we didn't hear him. But I can't. If nothing else, he's one of us. Something happened to him, and he's been wherever he is ever since the war started. *Awake.* I don't know about you, but I wouldn't want to be abandoned if someone had the choice."

Mind you, being trapped with Tor in a bunker for the rest of my life wouldn't have been the worst fate. I hadn't woken in our bunker; Tor had busted us out shortly after the firestorm of the war was over and taken my body to safety. But Cindra, Pax, and Oliver had, and from their pinched expressions, they remembered the feeling all too well.

"It's settled then," Fane said. "Let's start searching."

"What exactly are we searching for?" asked Grace. She looked eager and ready to help.

"Well, any entrance will be hidden. It'll probably be a bunker. Look for any natural feature, like a hill or a hollow—something that could be concealed," Oliver explained.

We split up to explore. Luckily for us, there were very few natural features in the area that could've hidden an entranceway. Within minutes we'd found it—the remains of what looked like an old, crumbled stone well, partially overgrown with spongy moss and the curling vines of an odd, twisting plant.

Set into the ground, the weathered metal door looked undisturbed, the moss encroaching over the control panel and around the spokes of the wheel. We set to work, tearing the grass up by the roots and clearing away the artfully placed debris.

"This looks like our bunker, doesn't it, Pax?" Cindra asked him once we'd exposed the entire door. He nodded, uncharacteristically solemn. "Did yours look the same?"

she asked Oliver and me.

"Tor had moved me by the time I woke up," I said. "And Oliver blew his up."

Cindra snorted as Oliver glared at me. "That doesn't surprise me."

Oliver tugged on the door wheel, trying his luck, but it wouldn't turn. He swore under his breath and prodded at a few random keys on the control pad. When it lit up, he swore again, this time in surprise.

"It actually still works. But since it's completely intact, we're going to need the code." He typed in several strings of numbers then sighed. "You guys may as well make yourself comfortable. This is going to take a few minutes. Unless, Pax, you can come somehow see what code we used to get in?"

Pax shook his head. "Sorry."

"No worries, it was a long shot. Right, kids, settle down and let me work my magic."

"I'll help," Fane offered, and the two of them set to work.

Cindra and I found a spot in the grass free of the twisting plants and leaned back against a large rock. Cindra closed her eyes.

"I'm going to leave some more of my notes," Pax said. "I brought a bunch of them with me. I won't go far," he said before we could protest. He wandered off, searching for a good hiding place.

"Cindra, I'm going to see if I can connect with Tor again."

"Okay," she murmured, already half asleep. "I might have a little nap."

Tor's familiar thread was easy to find among the others, the flicker replaced by a steadier glow. I took a deep breath and followed it.

13

TOR

I must still have been sedated, because everything was slightly fuzzy and slow, like I was trying to move through water. They'd put me in her room. In the bed that still smelled of her. I ran my fingers down the rose-gold walls and tried to remember.

The last time we'd been in this room together, I'd sat next to her, willing her to wake up, and not for the first time. Umbra's virus had infected all of us, but it had hit Ailith the hardest, and she'd hovered between life and death, oblivious to the chaos around her. Or so we'd thought. When she'd woken, we fought because I'd let Kalbir live after killing her father. Our last words in this room had been of anger and resentment, and so many other things were left unsaid.

And now she was gone. I'd imagined life without her before, and it had hurt. But now that she was dead, there was no pain. There was nothing, just a vast, hollow space. The pain was still there, I was sure of it, lingering at the edges and waiting for its chance to pounce. When it finally did, I would be glad. I needed to feel something to honor her, even if it killed me.

The framed picture of her and her family still stood on the dresser next to the bed, and I cradled it against my chest, ignoring the sharp edges of the frame. In it, she stood with her family, all now dead. Her face was reddened from too much sun, and her smile wide and slightly crooked. She looked present, fully in her time and place. The girl in the picture was not the woman I knew, but the soft new seed before it had hardened under layers of chaff.

Most of her clothes were still here, so I pulled a few of the softer things out of the drawers and piled them on the bed. I lay on my side and wrapped my arms around her pillow, letting the sedative pull me down into it. I could pretend she was here. I shouldn't, but just for a moment, I couldn't deny myself.

The day she'd awoken, when I'd looked into her eyes for the first time. I'd already been in love with her for years by then.

The first time we'd kissed, the air coppery from the deer she'd killed.

The first time we'd made love, the taste of her mingled with poisoned water.

The last time, the desperation of it, as though we'd known it would be the last. That the end was coming.

The door opened.

"Enjoying yourself?" Kalbir stood in the doorway, a smirk curling her lips as she took in the jumble of sheets and t-shirts.

"Why did you put me here? Why not in my own room?" I already knew the answer. Kalbir was a formidable woman, but she did have a spiteful streak.

"I thought this would be more amusing," she said, barely concealing her mirth.

"Go away, Kalbir." I turned my back to her and hugged the

picture frame again.

"*That's no way to talk to your best friend.*" *Her footsteps on the carpet were soft, like a cat's. A feral, hungry cat with very sharp teeth.*

"*You're not my friend.*" Stop answering her. Just ignore her, and she'll get bored and go away.

"*I'm the closest thing you've got, Tor.*"

I couldn't help it. I turned back to face her. "*Why are you here? Did Ethan finally get tired of you?*"

"*Don't be ridiculous. He knows when he's onto a good thing.*" *She grinned, running her tongue over her teeth.*

"*I'm sure he does.*" *I rolled my shoulders, cracking the bones in my neck with a savage pleasure.* "*Why am I still here? Why continue to drug me?*" *My voice grew louder as my irritation broke through.* Stop. Don't give her the satisfaction.

She was satisfied. She leaned back, triumphant. "*You're not going anywhere.*"

"*But I thought you wanted me to retrieve Fane? I can hardly do that here, doped up to my eyeballs,*" *I pointed out.*

"*Don't worry, you're serving your purpose as we speak. Now that we've let you be conscious enough, anyway. I'm sure he's on his way here.*"

What did that mean? *By "retrieve," I'd assumed she'd meant that I was to go after him.* "*Why would Fane come here? He knows Ethan is after him, and he knows what he'll do to him. He'd never be that stupid. Or that sentimental. It's not like we were the best of friends.*" *It was true. I respected Fane, admired him, even. But his interest in Ailith had made things complicated. Though looking back now, it seemed ridiculous. The jealousy that had spurred me into attacking him was gone. I just wished she'd lived to see it.*

"*No, you're right, he wouldn't be. Although, he is pretty damn sentimental for a machine.*"

"*Better not let Ethan hear you say that.*"

"*Don't steal my thunder, Tor. What I was going to say is that he wouldn't, but* she *would.*"

The drugs had confused me more than I'd thought. Couldn't make sense of what she was saying. "She? Cindra?"

Kalbir glanced at the doorway then dropped her voice to a conspiratorial whisper. "I'm not supposed to tell you this… But seeing how you can't do anything about it—and also to prove to you that I'm not the monster you think I am—you're bait, Tor. Ailith is alive. Fane goes where Ailith goes. And we both know she'll come for you."

Shel,

I don't know where you are. I made it back from the mainland to find you and you were gone. Whatever happened here…I can't stay. I'm going to find a boat and go to Dione Island. If you find this, please, come there. I promise I'll be there. I just wish it wasn't so dark. I love you.

Jen.

14
AILITH

Relief blossomed in my chest. *He knows I'm alive.* Being inside him, feeling the void I'd left behind, was like walking naked into a desert storm, stinging shards of memory and loss peeling away my skin then my flesh then even my bones, until nothing was left.

What would he do now? *Please be smart, Tor. Play along, wait for us.* As drugged as he was, I didn't think he had many choices. It had been difficult to understand his thoughts through the haze of sedatives at first, but the rawness of his emotions had been painfully clear.

"Is Tor okay?" Cindra asked. She'd rolled over onto her side and was watching me, her head propped on her hand.

"Yes… No… But at least he knows I'm alive." *What*

would be worse for him? Thinking I was dead, or knowing I was purposefully walking into a trap. For him.

She let out a long breath. "I'm glad, Ailith. I… It was awful when he brought you back. I've never seen anyone as broken."

I didn't want to know. The thought of his grief was almost more than I could bear. Tor and I had had only each other in the beginning, and that had bound us as tightly as our encoded bond. A world without him was not something I could understand, and he would feel the same.

Oliver and Fane still huddled by the bunker, Oliver rubbing his forehead as though trying to open the door with his mind.

"Where's Pax?"

"Over there." Cindra tilted her head toward where Pax sat idly playing with some of the twisted grass. He gazed far off into the distance, into another time and place.

"It must be so strange for him, traveling down all those future paths," Cindra remarked. "I wonder what it's like. Do you think it's like when you see the past?"

"I don't think so. I see…almost ghosts, I guess. Fragments of images of things that were there or that happened. But I see them outside of myself, like pale holograms. Everything Pax sees happens in his mind."

Although Pax and I shared a unique two-way link, I'd only ever seen one of his futures, and then, only when he'd remembered it for me.

Different emotions flitted across his face as we watched. Wonder, fear, understanding.

"Yeah, I bet it's incredible. It's just a shame it's not a bit more concise," I grumbled.

"He feels bad about it, you know," she said.

"Bad about what?" I'd always tried not to put too much pressure on Pax to use his ability to guide us—the variables simply evolved too fast, and there was nothing he could do to change that.

"About not being able to help you more with making decisions or telling you what's going to happen and so on. I know he feels responsible for some of the things that have happened. And guilty, although he'd never want us to know."

"He shouldn't feel that way. And I hope I haven't *made* him feel that way. Believe me, I know what it's like to have unpredictable abilities. I never fully understand what I see either."

"That's odd," Oliver said.

"What is?" Cindra and I stood, pulling out blades of grass that had twisted their way into our clothes.

"Well, it's a Cyborgist code signature, but it looks like it's been tampered with."

"What do you think that means?" Cindra asked.

"I have no idea." He looked troubled, unusual for him.

"Can you open it?" I asked.

"We already have." Fane gave the wheel an experimental turn, and the locking mechanism groaned and slid in response. A series of rasping movements later, the seal on the door gave way with an exasperated grunt. "Are you ready?"

No. If I never went down into a bunker again, it would be too soon. I could tell from the others' faces that they felt the same.

Fane didn't wait for a response. A hiss and a whoosh, and the door opened into darkness.

***

"At least my bunker had stairs," Oliver grumbled as we

descended the ladder cautiously, our hands slick on the smooth rungs. The air was stale but held no other odors, and I allowed myself to relax a little. After we'd all cleared the ladder and stepped onto the pressed concrete floor, a sound echoed from somewhere down below, so faint it was nearly inaudible.

"Can anyone else hear that?" I asked. We all held our breath. Nothing but cold silence and the sensation of the earth pressing all around us.

And the rumble of Pax's stomach.

"Sorry," he whispered. There was a rustle as he pulled a packet from his pocket.

"Pax!"

"Sorry," he mumbled again, chewing with exaggerated slowness. Fane suppressed a grin. My nerves were so tightly strung I wanted to knock their heads together.

"What did you think you heard?" Cindra asked.

"It was music," Fane said. "I heard it too."

"Should we make some noise or something? What if we spook William or whoever else is down there?" I asked.

"Yeah, but do we really want to give them a heads up?" Oliver challenged. "It might be better to catch them off their guard."

"Not if we want him to trust us. William is one of us, Oliver, and we *are* looking for allies," I reminded him. "He might be more inclined to become one if we don't go sneaking up on him. The man's been down here for *years*."

Oliver gave an irritated sigh. "Suit yourself, then."

The faint echo began again.

"William?" I called. The echo stopped.

"He knows we're here," I whispered.

At the end of the domed tunnel was another door. A keypad similar to the one outside was mounted on the wall next to it. "Shit. Do you think we'll need another code?"

The thought of waiting here in the tunnel underground while Oliver fumbled with another lock pulled my nerves even tighter.

Oliver typed in a combination, and the lock clicked back. "Nope. It looks like the internal code is the same as ours." Surprise warred with the smugness in his voice. "Ready?"

We'd let whoever was on the other side of the door know we were here and given them a chance to prepare. *Whoever William turns out to be, I hope he's willing to listen first. Maybe Oliver was right.* It was too late now.

"Let me go through first," Fane said.

Oliver bowed and stood aside as Fane opened the door and stepped into the room. For a couple of heartbeats, we heard nothing then Fane said: "You may as well come in."

We filed through the doorway and into the main room of the bunker. The space was small, similar to the ones the others had woken up in, except for one thing.

The bunker was pristine, as though no one had ever been there. And maybe no one had. The room was empty.

"What the fuck? There's no one here," Oliver said, all smugness gone.

"William?" I called again, louder than before.

"What? Like he's hiding under the bed?" Oliver asked snidely before shrugging and dropping to his knees to have a look.

I checked William's thread—it was there, brighter than before.

"He's definitely here," Pax and I said at the same time.

"Well, where is he then?"

"It doesn't look like this bunker's been used. Could it be a fake, like the mineshaft at the compound?" Cindra asked.

Oliver shrugged "It's worth a try. Fane? Any super-robot powers? Infrared? Sonar?"

"No. Unfortunately, they made me as human as possible. In this situation, I'm as completely incompetent as you are." His smile as Oliver glared at him was benign.

We started searching for another door, tracing our fingers over the walls and the floor, looking for anything that seemed out of place. Nothing.

"It's a tiny room. How could we miss it?" I asked Grace as she stood next to me.

"You…the others…you lived in a place like this? For years?"

"Not exactly," I replied. "We were asleep. Pax, Cindra, and Oliver woke up in theirs, but they escaped shortly afterward. Tor took me out of ours long before I ever woke up."

"Tor stayed with you? Even though it was dangerous? He could've left you, and he didn't?" Her voice was wistful.

Yes, he did. "He's a good man," I said.

"I wish he…that I knew a man like him," she replied.

"I'm sure you will, one day," I said. *Awkward.*

She looked at me for a long moment then started to speak. "I—"

A crash from the closet cut her off.

"I think I found something," Pax called.

Grace flashed me a half-smile and looked away.

Pax was right—the back of the closet was false. After some yanking and cursing from Oliver, we slid it aside to reveal a long, sloping hallway. Motion lights flickered along the floor at intermittent points, guiding us to yet another door at the far end. A *sealed* door. Oliver's shoulders slumped.

"Let's try it the old-fashioned way this time," I said. I knocked on it. "William? Are you there?" No answer. I changed tack. "William, we *know* you're there. We're not here to hurt you. We're like you." I looked at the others, getting only shrugs in return.

I tried again. "I'm Pantheon Modern Cyborg Program Omega, cyborg number O-117-9791. Hello?"

"Hello?" A tentative voice spoke from the other side of the door. *Not* William's voice. I shook my head at the others.

Oliver didn't get the hint. "Yeah, are you William? Look, mate, we—" He stopped as I waved my hands.

There was a faint hissing, and we stepped back, expecting the door to unlock and swing open.

Instead, my face began to feel strange, like I was wearing someone else's skin. I reached up to touch it and couldn't feel my fingers. Around me, the others were doing the same.

It was a trap.

"Get out. *Get out!*" I pushed Grace back the way we'd come. Fane reached the door first, yanking on it so hard I thought he would tear it off its hinges.

It didn't move. Fane looked down at his hands with an expression so bewildered it would've been comical in another situation.

The hissing continued over our heads through a small vent near the top of the corridor. "There!" I pointed. "That vent. Something's coming through. We have to—" I staggered. "We—" *Something. We have to do something.* My hand slid uselessly off the wall as I fell to my knees. "Pax—"

"It'll be okay, Ailith. We have to go this way. We have to—" His eyes rolled back as he passed out.

"Why does this keep happening?" Oliver muttered as his head dropped to his chest. "Why—"

The last thing I saw was Fane's terrified face in an all-too-human struggle not to submit. He lost the struggle, and so did I.

Cindra,

If you're reading this, I'm sorry. I know it wasn't my fault, but I'm sorry because I want you to always be happy. My mother used to tell me that was impossible, that nobody can be happy all the time. I suppose it's true. In case something happened to him, and to me, he wanted me to make sure you knew how much he loved you. He told me that you saved him, that you fixed something in him that broke the day he was born. He didn't write this himself because he thought he would do it wrong. I told him I would do it wrong too, but he said even if I did, you would understand.

Pax.

15
AILITH

"Drink, madam?"

Two waiters stood before me, both offering a golden tray of crystal flutes filled with a pale liquid so sparkling it blinded me.

I blinked.

The two waiters merged into one. "Drink, madam?" he repeated.

I shut my eyes again and counted to five before opening them.

"Are you all right, madam?" He was still there, leaning forward and eying me quizzically. He was an older man with heavy jowls, his meager hair neatly parted and combed over his spotted scalp. He was dressed formally in a black suit with a buttoned-down white shirt and blue bowtie.

"Where am I?" I asked him. I tried to think back. *The hallway. Hissing. Fane, afraid.* He was never afraid. "Where are the others?" My voice came out feeble and pathetic.

"Perhaps madam has already imbibed enough this evening." He jowls wobbled with mirth as he held the tray out of my reach.

"Where are the others?" I ground out, my voice gaining strength as I tried to step forward. *I can't move.* Only my hands seemed to be loose.

"Why, they're here, of course." He gave a shallow bow from his waist and stepped aside, gesturing elegantly with his white-towel-draped arm.

Nearly everything in the room was blue. All through the vast room, strangers milled and mingled in front of cerulean tapestries under soaring sapphire-blue arches, chatting to one another as they quaffed the effervescent liquid and plucked morsels of food off cobalt tables. Their clothing was odd, made from rich, formal fabrics tailored into strangely infantile designs, all in shades of blue. An orchestra sat against one wall, a lilting childish lullaby rising and falling from their instruments.

The partygoers wore masks…at least, I hoped they were masks. Modeled after human infants, they each had an exaggerated feature—obscenely large, wet-looking lips, bald, blue-veined pates, corpulent, fleshy cheeks that obscured their eyes. The braziers burning around the room distorted the shadows playing over them.

Waiters like the one before me wove in and out of the crowds, disappearing into one group and appearing out the other side, their trays empty. *I must be dreaming.* I pressed fingernails into my palms to wake myself up as the melody of the music taunted me.

"The others I came here with. Where are they?" My voice rose, and several of the guests turned to look at me. A woman whose mask had two elongated bottom teeth tilted her head and giggled.

My head was held fast by a weighted band, but from the corner of my eye, I made out what looked a smooth metal frame lined with blue padding, like a coffin.

My waiter friend leaned in again. "If madam would like to join the party, I suggest she lower her voice. We expect our guests to be on their best behavior."

"Guest? I'm not a guest. I'm a prisoner—"

"Madam," he warned, and his voice changed, becoming rough and uncultured. "I could always *remove* you."

"Ailith?"

"Pax? Oh my god, you're alive. Where are you? What the hell is going on?"

"I'm here, at the party. The food's not real."

"What?" I choked back a hysterical laugh. Only Pax could wake up in this situation and be thinking about the food. His normalcy was like a slap in the face. *Think, Ailith. Pax is alive. The others might be too. Play along. "Pax, I'm coming to find you."*

"I'm so sorry," I said, giving the waiter my most apologetic smile. "I'm not accustomed to such extravagant affairs. I'm afraid it's gone to my head a bit. But I'm fine now."

He eyed me suspiciously. "Are you sure? We don't tolerate uncouth behavior here."

"I promise. I would like to rejoin the party, please."

For a moment, it seemed as though he was going to refuse then he sighed and moved his arm off to the side, out of my sight.

"I'll trust you, madam, but if I see any signs of your former vulgarity, I shall eject you from the venue."

There was a click, and the weight on my forehead disappeared. I tested my arms and legs and found I could move them again. "Thank you—?"

"Arnold," he replied, bowing again. "Oh. And please leave your mask on." His smile was benign, but his tone was heavy with threat.

"I will, thank you. *Arnold.*" I inclined my head graciously. "Excuse me." As I moved away from him toward the dazzling crowd, I glanced back. Arnold stood in front of a tall metal capsule. Just before its door closed, I caught sight of metallic restraints where my head, arms, and legs had been. As I watched, the pod wavered then turned into a viridian marble column, indistinguishable from the others that surrounded the room. He saw me looking and smiled.

Shit. Don't panic, I reprimanded myself. *Just look for the others.* But where to begin?

"Pax? Are you still here?"

"Of course, where else would I be?"

"I'm coming to find you."

"I'm over by the buffet table."

"Of course you are. Don't move."

"How will I recognize you? What are you wearing?"

"What? I'm—" I looked down at myself. The cargo trousers and t-shirt I'd been wearing earlier were gone. In their place was a fine linen gown, the soft sky-blue of forget-me-nots. It hung in loose folds, weighted by the heavy embroidery around the hem. I smoothed my hands over the fabric. It felt odd—tangible, but not quite real.

I raised my hands to my face, my fingertips just grazing the mask Arnold had ordered me not to remove. My cheeks were plump, framing a wide, toothless hole. I slipped my hand under the edge of my grinning gums, relieved to find my real face still underneath.

I contemplated the crowd. Maybe none of this was real, but then what the hell was it? Keeping my back to as few people as possible, I inched along the wall toward the buffet table at the far side. Halfway, my path was blocked by a heavy-set woman suckling a near-emaciated man, liquid spilling down his chin and soaking the front of her dress.

As I skirted them in disgust, a massive, black grandfather clock, the only non-blue object in the room, started to chime.

I wrote earlier that I would tell you more about the others when our story was closer to its end, because history has a way of changing people. The way you see them now wasn't always the way they were.

I met Oliver first as a foe then made my life with him. Oliver was born into troubled times. He survived an abusive mother and a father who took his own life while holding his young son's hand, only to be deemed unacceptable by his peers for the roughness these events marked him with. The culmination of these things bred in him a kind of psychopathy that enabled him to do many things he later regretted, although many were his duty at the time. This viciousness further alienated him, trapping him in a malicious cycle.

He became a cyborg as a last-ditch attempt at acceptance. Who knows how his efforts would've paid off without the war? Yet, he embraced his new state in the end, risking his life for it, and for us. The war was the making of him. All the traits scorned by his peers became his ability to survive, albeit in ways others deemed callous and even inhuman at times. But eventually, the aftermath calmed something in him, and those traits withered and crumbled away, leaving behind something sensitive and new.

—Cindra, Letter to Omega

16
AILITH

The moment the last chime sounded, a palpable ripple swept the room. The arches and the tapestries, the stained-glass windows, the guests' clothes—the blue leached out, replaced by varying shades of purple. The guests' faces had also changed; enormous violet eyes with bottomless, dilated pupils, broad, flattened noses squished between rosy cheeks, and tiny chins with points so sharp they could've drawn blood looked back at me.

I glanced down at myself, and sure enough, I was now swathed in frilly lavender replete with pansy-hued lace and ribbons. My mask had also changed, now featuring an outsized cherub's mouth. The band struck up a bouncing, playful tune.

I needed to find Pax. Then we had to locate the others. I continued toward the buffet table, dodging the crowd, who were now spinning, and dancing, and chasing each other in a caricature of tag. Once a target was caught, the players fell to the floor, writhing together in awkwardly simulated intimacy.

I made it to the table unmolested and searched amongst the various meats and pastries for Pax. "*Pax? I'm at the buffet table. I'm wearing—*" What? A purple dress? "*I've got my hand on my head,*" I finished lamely, placing my palm on top of my pig-tailed hair. All around me, a dozen other guests laughed and did the same. *Shit.*

"*Okay. I'm putting my hands on my hips.*" My dozen shadows followed suit. "Would you kindly fuck off?" I ask the woman closest to me. As she gazed back at me with her immense blank eyes, her mask wobbled, and tears glistened on her neck.

"Ailith, I'm here," Pax said from behind me.

I spun to find a man with giant rosy cheeks that obscured the rest of his features. "Oh, thank goodness." I grabbed his arm and propelled him to the closest pillar.

"Pax, what the actual hell is going on? What is this place?"

He pondered for a minute. "I have no idea. This…wasn't anything I've seen. It must've been another blind spot."

Great. Every so often, there were gaps in Pax's ability, where he couldn't see what was coming next. He called it a crossroads, and it usually meant something crucial was going to happen.

"We've got to find the others," I said. "Then we'll figure a way out of here." How long had we even been here?

"Can you see where they are? Like, through their own eyes?"

Duh. Why hadn't I thought of that? I closed my eyes under my mask and concentrated. The closest thread to mine was Cindra's. "Keep watch, Pax," I murmured and slid down it. I was inside her. She was…standing at the edge of a sea of purple. Everything I saw through her eyes looked the same as the view from mine. *Look down. Please, Cindra, look down.* If I could see what kind of dress she was wearing, we could find her easily. She didn't.

"Damn," I swore, frustrated. "She's on the edge of the crowd, like us, but everything looks the same."

"Can you see us?" Pax asked. "I'll wave."

I searched the crowd. "Yes. We're…directly across the room from her. Quick, if we cut through the crowd, we'll be able to reach her." I slid back down the thread and into my own body.

Pax hesitated. "I don't know if that's a good idea."

"What? Why not? It's the quickest way. If we go around the room, we might lose her."

"I don't know *why*. It's just a feeling."

Several heads turned toward us.

"Pax, we need to go. Blend in. *Now.*" I grabbed his hands, skipping around in a circle. The celebrants watching us clapped in joy and mimicked us. Soon, most of the room was twirling. We merged with the other dancers as we spun toward the spot where I hoped Cindra would be.

As soon as we cleared the press of bodies on the other side of the dance floor, I dropped Pax's hands and searched. There were only two people not dancing, a woman with long, dark braided pigtails in ruffled mauve, and a man who seemed to be soiling himself.

We sidled up to the woman, trying to look casual. I stood next to her and said her name, quietly enough that no one else would hear. "Cindra?" *Please be Cindra.*

She turned her head sharply. Her mask displayed a tiny mouth distorted by a row of widely-spaced teeth the size of my hand "Ailith? Oh, thank god. I've been looking for everyone. Have you found anyone else?"

"Pax," I replied. "He's right here." I tugged on his sleeve.

"What is this place?" Cindra asked.

"I have no idea, but we need to get the hell out of here. We need to—" As I spoke, the great clock at the end of the room chimed again. Like before, at the last chime, a gust passed over the crowd, and green permeated the room along with a throbbing, tribal beat.

"Wow, Ailith, nice boobs," Cindra said.

I looked down. I was now clad in deep, iridescent green the color of a peacock's feather, a plunging neckline giving my cleavage more credit than it deserved. "You too," I replied, indicating the sheer lime fabric of her own outfit. "I can see your nipples."

She stared down at her breasts, horrified. "Those aren't my breasts! Mine are much more—"

"I wish I'd gotten nicer clothes," Pax lamented. "This is the third tuxedo I've worn. The third in my whole life, actually."

"What does my face look like now?" I asked. As repulsed as I was by whatever was going on, I was also curious. And for now, at least, we didn't seem to be in any danger.

"You could cut glass on your cheekbones." She laughed. "And Pax, you have a hideous mustache. Me?"

"You've got massive red lips, parted like they're begging for—"

"Canape?" a waiter asked, shoving a tray between us.

As we looked around, the crowd's behavior changed. Where before they'd been gamboling like children, now their movements were sensuous, their bodies writhing against one another. The previous giddiness that had lit the purple room was gone, replaced by a frantic, almost ominous air. The smells of sweat and sex rose from the crowd as their motions grew ever more fevered.

"Um, let's take a step back," Cindra said, and we moved behind the pillar in unison.

"That took a bit of a turn, didn't it?" I said, no longer laughing.

"I feel like we're hurtling toward something," Pax added. "But I'm not sure what."

"I know what you mean." Cindra touched the myrtle-green brocade closest to us. "It feels so real. But it can't be, right? It reminds me of something. All these people…the changing colors. The fact that's there's no exit or entrance…"

"There *isn't?*" I hadn't noticed; I'd been too concerned with looking for the others. Tor would be ashamed of me. "Are you s—"

A scuffle broke out behind another pillar a few yards down from us. A laughing group of men in leering masks had surrounded a young woman and were advancing on her, their hands grabbing at the front of her dress. She

tripped over her hem as she scrambled backward toward a
wall. As she fell, her mask slipped up and revealed part of
her face, pale and terrified.

Grace.

As with Oliver, the war and its aftermath set something free in Tor, something good. While others' scars stayed tender, laced with guilt and haunting them until the end of their days, Tor's cleansed him. He was able to finally fight for something, for himself, and for those who loved him, something he'd turned his back on before. But the war allowed him a clean slate, enabled him to eventually put away his regrets and pay his penance. I was unsure of him at first, so still and aloof on the outside, yet with a roiling wildness just underneath the skin. Yet I grew to love his subtle kindness, his fierceness tempered with an innate gentleness.

—Cindra, Letter to Omega

17
AILITH

"Grace!" I shouted, my voice lost in the pounding music and delighted moans. As I raced toward her, a couple fell across my path, the man's pants around his ankles as he rode between the woman's thighs. She grabbed at me as I strode past them, my feet tangling in the hem of the dress that pooled over her shoulder.

"No, thank you," I said tartly. The woman didn't seem to care, moaning deeply and grabbing the man's hair as she came.

I tapped the closest man on the shoulder. "What the fuck do you think you're doing?"

"Here's another one, boys," he said, rubbing his hands together with delight.

I ignored him. "Grace, it's me, Ailith." At the sound of my voice, she let out a loud sob. "Come over to me, Grace. Don't worry about them." Her dress was torn at the shoulder, but she seemed unhurt.

"Where do you think you're going?" one of the men asked her as she scrambled to her feet. He grabbed her upper arm.

"Let me go," she blurted. "Get your hands off me."

"What's wrong? We're having a party, sweetling. Don't you want to celebrate? I can show you a good time." He gyrated his hips suggestively.

"Grace, come here," I repeated. "Ignore him."

She did as I said, wrenching her arm away and sprinting past the other three men.

"Now then," the man said to me. "If you're going to spoil our fun, you're going to have to take her place."

I felt, rather than saw, Cindra and Pax materialize at my back. "That's not going to happen," I replied. "Grace, are you all right?"

Grace was *not* all right. She was frightened. And pissed off. "I'll rip your dick off," she shrieked, emboldened by the three cyborgs at her back. She flew toward the man who'd grabbed her, her fingernails clawing for the eyes of his mask. He raised his hands to block her, but she was too quick, and, with a sharp tug, yanked his mask off. It was his turned to be shocked. The face that stared back at us was…so normal. Sandy hair, just a hint of a mustache, and pale brown eyes that darted around the room in a panic.

The music stopped. Even the cacophony of moans switched off, as though someone had hit the mute button. The man dropped to his knees. "No, no. Please, *no*." The crowd advanced on us, forming a circle around the prostrate man.

"No one is to remove their mask," a voice boomed out over the silent crowd. "No one is *ever* to remove their mask."

The man pressed his forehead to the floor as he continued to grovel. "Please, it wasn't my fault—"

"Step back," I murmured to Grace, and the four of us melted into the crowd. I gripped Grace's hand until it became stuck to mine with nervous sweat.

The crowd parted, and a man dressed all in white strode through to stand over the cowering figure. "You know what the penalty is for removing your mask."

That voice. William.

Besides the waiters, he was the only one in the room not wearing a mask, though a metal band encircled his neck. His face was bare, a narrow, pale oval that made his eyes seem too large. His dark blond hair had been raggedly cut, accentuating his pointed chin and full, almost feminine mouth. He looked like a painting of an angel who'd fallen down a hole to Hell.

"Get up," he demanded.

The man whimpered into the jade-tiled floor.

William sighed. He leaned over and grabbed the man by the hair then jerked his head back and forced him onto his heels. The man hung limply in William's hands, his head lolling against his chest as sobs wracked his body. The crowd wailed.

As the crowd's howls climbed in pitch, William leaned over and spoke into the man's ear, just loud enough for me to hear. "Please. Don't make this any worse for me. You know how much I hate this." The man sniffled. "You know you'll come back." The man took a deep breath and nodded once in acquiescence.

William straightened and addressed the crowd. "Those

who remove their masks must pay the price." The throng of partygoers, some of whom were only partially dressed, began to keen, a high-pitched howl that sent chills up my spine. A long, pale-bladed dagger materialized in William's right hand, and he drew his arm back.

"It's better this way," he muttered. "You know what happens at the end." He thrust his arm forward, piercing the man's chest with the dagger as the mob screeched. The pointed tip emerged from the man's back, his blood beading on the polished blade. He gasped and looked up at William, a slight smile curling his lips. William twisted the blade and drove it in further.

The man slumped over the hilt, and the crowd rushed forward, swarming around William and the dead man, obscuring them. The ebony clock chimed, and a classical melody rose from the strings of the orchestra. The now silent, orange-clad mob stepped back, and William raised his hands.

"Please, enjoy the evening. Feast, dance…whatever. For as you know, death comes to us all," he intoned as though by rote, rolling his eyes. As his voice carried through the room, the revelers paired off, circling across the floor in a somber waltz. He turned, disappearing into the crowd. The man's body was gone, leaving no trace that he'd ever existed.

"William!" I called after him. *"William!"* But he'd disappeared, lost in the swirling autumn hues. I turned back to the others. "I think that was William."

"I don't think he's the ally we're looking for, Ailith. Not after what he just did," Cindra said.

The way he'd spoken to the man before he'd killed him. "I'm not so sure," I replied. "There's more going on here than we understand." *But even so, it was a mistake to come here. My mistake.*

Grace stood with her fist stuffed into her mouth under her mask. Exaggerated purple bags hung from the eyes of her disguise, and her peach dress was almost matronly. She backed away from us, shaking her head, and into a small orangewood table holding an amber-crystal vase of torch lilies. The vase wobbled then fell, toppling over the edge of the table and into the hands of a stranger whose mask wore a crooked grimace of stained yellow teeth.

Grace's shriek was drowned out by the orchestra, and she crouched to the ground, holding her head. The stranger deftly balanced the vase back on the table and held up both hands.

"It's okay. It's me, Oliver. I saw the commotion and figured if there was any trouble, you lot had to be at the center of it."

Cindra nearly knocked the lilies over again as she rushed into his arms. "Oliver, I-I'm so glad to see you." Her voice broke.

"Well, this is a bit of a shitshow, isn't it? I mean, even for us. Do any of you know what the hell's going on?" He narrowed his eyes at Pax and me. "Who's that? Ailith? And I'd recognize Pax's beanpole body anywhere." We nodded, our oversized heads bobbing grotesquely.

"And that's Grace." I pointed to the floor where Grace still sat. She'd calmed down a bit once she'd realized it was Oliver, but she still wasn't ready to stand.

"So no ideas?" he asked again. "Have we just fallen down the rabbit hole? And what the hell happened to that guy?"

"I think the man in white was William," I replied. "But I have no idea what the rest of it—"

"I think I know," Cindra interrupted. I couldn't see her face, but she sounded choked, like she was going to throw up. "*The Masque of the Red Death.*"

"I'm sorry, what?" Oliver sounded as confused as I was.

"*The Masque of the Red Death*," Cindra repeated. "By Edgar Allan Poe."

Oliver shook his head. "No idea? Ailith? Pax?"

"Nope."

Cindra sighed loudly. "I know it's an old book, but you all should really start reading."

"Cindra, if we make it out of here alive, I promise you, I'll read everything you put in my hands. But right now, just tell us what the hell you *think* is going on. Because anything called *Masque of the Red Death* can't be good."

"The story was first published in 1842—" she began.

"Cindra, I love how much you love stories, but please, give us the short version. No themes, no symbolism…just tells us the bad news," Oliver chided her.

"Sorry. Okay, so basically, in the *Masque of The Red Death*, the people are sealed away at a party with seven rooms, each one a different color: blue, purple, green, orange, white, violet, and black. The colors are thought to symbolize the different stages of life. For example—"

"Cindra," Oliver reminded her.

"Sorry," she said again. "We're now in the orange room. That means there are only two rooms left until the black room."

"What happens in the black room?" I asked. "Or can I guess?"

"You can probably guess. The Red Death appears in the black room as a blood-soaked specter that slaughters every single guest."

We were silent. Refined laughter drifted from the dance floor.

"So when this room turns black, we're all going to die?" Oliver asked.

Grace wailed from her spot on the floor.

"Well, that's how the story plays out in Poe's work," Cindra replied.

"Oh, for fuck's sake," Oliver said and began to lift the edge of his mask.

"Oliver, don't!" I shrieked and leaped over Grace to tug the mask back over his chin. "You saw what happened."

"Fuck," he said again, his voice shaky.

Cindra squeezed his hand. "I know we're more resilient than most, love, but let's try to come up with a better plan."

"We need to find Fane. Oliver, have you seen him?"

"No," he replied. "Which is odd. I would've expected him to search for you."

"We need to find Fane first then we need a plan. Cindra? How many more rooms are there before the black room again?"

"Two," she said. "White and vio—"

The black clock struck again, and the responding ripple turned the room into a winter wonderland.

"One," Cindra said. "One more room before the Red Death."

Unlike the others, Pax's burden grew with the passage of time, and it took its toll. He wasn't always, as you know him now, so old in his mind. His ability was a terrible weight, one that wouldn't let him rest. And yet, early on, of all of us, Pax emerged the most unscathed. Perhaps because his world had ended long before when he'd lost his mother, the person who was everything to him. On the back of that loss, our lives in the aftermath were an adventure. His mind had always been surreal, the worlds and creatures he explored in his laboratory already separating his universe from others. It made me question if our abilities were as random as they claimed.

—Cindra, Letter to Omega

18

AILITH

I looked down. My marigold gown had transformed into folds of camellia-white brocade. "How can any of these be real?" I said. "I mean, *really* real. This can't just *happen*." We'd been so caught up in the illusion that we hadn't thought of it as anything but real. "I mean, these clothes, the rooms…and where did that man's body go?" I pointed to the spot where he'd fallen. "It couldn't have just disappeared, could it?"

"You're right," Oliver said. "I just—"

"I know, me too," I said. "It looks and feels real. But it can't be. Someone's behind this. We need to find Fane then

William."

"*William's* probably the one behind this, A."

"I'm not sure that he is, Oliver." I told him what William had said to the man before he'd killed him. "I think he might be caught up here, the same as we are."

"Maybe," Oliver said, sounding unconvinced. "Let's find Fane first then we'll deal with William."

"I'll wait with Grace," Cindra said. "And we'll stay right here, for as long as we can. We probably want to keep as low-key as possible."

"Agreed. I'll look for Fane. Oliver, see if you can figure out what's going on."

"I will. And we'll meet back here when that damned clock strikes again. Hurry," he said to me. "By my guess, we haven't got long."

I stood next to Cindra and Grace, closing my eyes under my mask and searching for Fane's thread. It blazed so brightly that I found it immediately and went through it. He was spinning in the arms of an ivory-tuxedoed man wearing a mask with a visage so lined his jowls rivaled Arnold's.

I pulled back then searched for that mask in the crowd. *There, in the middle of the dance floor.* In the man's delicate grasp was a taller, broader man in bone-colored attire, whose mask scowled under bushy grey eyebrows the thickness of my arm. *That has to be Fane.*

I wove through the crowd toward the pair, trying to keep rhythm with the dancers. When I reached them, I tapped the jowled man on the shoulder. "May I cut in?"

After a moment's hesitation, he bowed graciously and spun away into the throng. I took Fane's hands in mine and began to waltz, trying to remember what I'd been taught. *One, two three. One, two, three.*

"Fane?"

"Ailith?"

"Yes. Are you having a good time?" I asked, my voice acerbic.

He laughed. "Yes, actually. I was very flattered when he asked, and I don't know how to lead. I thought maybe it was a good time to learn."

"I've been trying to find everyone—you're the last. Did you not see the commotion earlier?"

"Yes."

"Well then, why didn't come and have a look? Oliver did—that's how we found him."

"I thought it was part of the celebration," he replied. "And then this good gentleman asked me to dance—"

"Do you not see that something's very wrong here?" I stopped dancing and glared at him.

"You know I can't see your face, right?" he asked. "But I'll assume that you're glaring."

"Fane, I just—" I threw up my hands in exasperation. "You understand our lives might be in danger, yes?"

"Yes, I do. And I figured the best way to minimize that danger was to blend in. Like we should be doing now." He inclined his head. Several of the dancers closest to us had paused, watching us.

Fane threw back his head and gave a hearty laugh, belying his mask's scowl. He pulled me close then twirled me away. The lingering couples' interest in us vanished, and they returned to their waltz.

"Do you have any idea what's behind all of this? I think that man in white was William. And Cindra has another theory." I repeated the story of the Red Death as we danced across the floor.

"So according to Cindra, we have one more room before these walls turn black and everyone dies?"

"Yes. Hence my sense of urgency."

"That's not a lot of time."

"Yes, Fane. I *know*."

He grinned. "Don't worry. We'll find a way out. We always do."

"So far," I grumbled. "But that's bound to only last so long. C'mon, let's meet up with the others and figure out a plan."

We whirled with purpose toward them. "Do you have any idea what this place is, Fane? Who these people are?" I kept my eye on the clock as we rotated, just waiting for it to strike.

"No. But there's something about them…"

"What do you mean?"

"When I was holding hands with that gentleman, he didn't quite feel…real."

"Not real?" I asked as an enthusiastic elbow caught me in ribs. The owner flashed me an apologetic smile as she jostled past. "Ouch. They *certainly* feel real. Still, I agree. There's no way they can be."

We reached the others without further incident. Grace had recovered enough to stand, but the white primrose woven into her hair shook with each breath.

"Any luck figuring out what's going on?" I asked Oliver.

"No," he said. "You?"

"I found Fane. But I haven't seen William." I'd kept an eye out for him on our way across the dance floor, but seeing as everyone present was now wearing white, I'd had no luck.

"William is our only lead at this point," Cindra said. "but I don't think we should split up to look for him. Can't you find him the same way you found me and Fane?"

"I can try." I found William's thread in the network and slid into him. I was surrounded by darkness and silence.

Something's gone wrong.

Then heavy cool air brushed over my lips and William opened his eyes. He was in the room he'd been in the night before, only this time, I was able to make out shapes in the gloom. He was surrounded by what seemed like hundreds of long, metallic tubes, dull gray in the shadow.

Someone's here. His heart pounded in his chest. *Real someones. Several of them. This could be it. My chance to end this. My* only *chance. Breathe, Will. You know what you have to do.* A giddy laugh burst from him, echoing around the chamber. He patted the closest cylinder and spoke aloud. "Okay, everyone, wish me luck." He closed his eyes again. *Good luck.*

I pulled back into myself. The sudden sea of white stung my eyes. "He's not here," I said, squinting at the others. "He's in another room. But I'm positive we'll see him again. From what I gathered, something *is* about to happen."

"Do you think he's on our side or not?" Cindra asked.

I hesitated. "I'm not sure. I *think* he is. He sees us as a chance for him to…stop whatever's going on here."

"That doesn't exactly mean he's with us, though, does it?" Oliver pointed out.

"I know. But we can't know for certain until we actually meet him."

"I don't think we'll have long to wait," Fane said. And he was right.

Without any ceremony, the ebony clock gave a resounding chime.

19

AILITH

A sigh swept the room as the violet dusk settled upon us. Our faces changed accordingly, becoming gaunt caricatures of the dying. My stiff brocade softened into drapes of vervain silk.

One chime left. We need to find William now.

The atmosphere in the room transformed, a pall settling over the crowd. They danced no longer, and as the orchestra struck up a mournful elegy, many of them began to weep.

"This doesn't bode well," Pax said. "And before you ask, no, I can't see what's to come. Only that we *can* make it out of here alive. And in some paths, we even *do*."

"Well, that's comforting. Thank you, Pax," Oliver said sourly.

Pax shrugged.

"William might be here now," I said, standing on my tiptoes and craning my neck to search the crowd. "Damn. Where is he?" I searched again for his thread and followed it. There. He was…right behind us.

I spun around. "William?" The others' masks turned in our direction.

He recoiled with a shocked expression. "You know my name?"

"Yes. I— Actually, it's a long story. We'll talk about it later. I get the feeling we're in danger. Am I right?"

"Yes," he said simply.

"From you?" Fane and the others had sidled into a silent formation, casually blocking his escape. Even Grace stood her ground, her hands balled into fists. *Good girl.*

"No!" he exclaimed, his eyes widening in alarm. He glanced furtively from side to side and dropped his voice. "Not from me. I'm trapped here. The same as you. When…that incident happened earlier, I saw you, knew you were different. It's becoming so hard for me to tell. That's why I came to find you. "

"What's going to happen?" Oliver asked.

"The Red Death," William replied. "It's—"

"We know what it is," I interrupted. "What we need to know is how we can stop it."

"You can't," he said. "Unless—"

"Unless *what,* Will? I don't want to sound impatient here, but I don't think we have a lot of time."

"Unless you kill the Red Death."

"Shocking," said Oliver. "It always seems to end that way. Okay, I'll bite. How do we kill the Red Death?"

"With this." Will scanned the room again then pressed what looked like a shiv into Oliver's hands.

"You're kidding." Oliver glanced down at what could only be called a whittled stick. "Are we fighting a vampire?"

"Of course not," Will said. "But it was the best I could do."

"Why can't you do it?" Oliver asked him.

"I have a role to play. I—" He blanched suddenly and darted away into the crowd.

Arnold was making his way toward us, a disapproving look on his flaccid face.

"Oliver, hide that stick. Everybody else, get wailing," I whispered frantically.

Cindra threw her head back and gave an unsettling howl then flung herself into my arms. Pax and the others followed suit, and by the time Arnold reached us, we were all but beating our breasts and rending our clothes. He scrutinized us for a few moments then, seemingly satisfied, passed us by.

"Is he gone?" I asked.

A tension gripped the air. The dirge of the celebrants rose, climbing ever higher until I had to clap my hands over my ears. *That sound could drive a person mad.*

The clock struck, a single reverberating chime, echoing throughout the chamber.

As we stood rooted to the spot, the crowd milled like a herd of cattle in the center of the dancefloor. Inky darkness, deeper than black, seeped into the floor at one end of the room. It advanced slowly, permeating the walls and floor as it passed, while a deep crimson snaked up the tables and chairs, the riot of violet flowers turning to dust in the now-scarlet vases.

The Red Death had come.

Screams of pure terror filled the room, turning my bones to jelly as the revelers tried to run from the spreading shadow. They huddled together at the far end, their screams melting into sobs and impassioned prayers.

"Remember, it can't be real," Fane said.

I know it's not real. But what if? What if? We stood our ground as the blackness spread under our feet, obscuring the mallow tiles, the muscles along my spine twitching as I held myself still. It reached the far end and climbed the walls.

When it had filled the last corner of the ceiling, a door appeared at the opposite end to the horrified cluster.

And through the door came Death.

When I began to write to you about Ailith, I found I struggled. How very strange, to be unable to describe the person who arguably played the largest role in our story. She never wanted to become a cyborg—she only wanted to live. And yet, she became so much bigger than her own life. Perhaps it's because she was all of us at one time or another that, although this is our story, it's her story to tell.

—Cindra, Letter to Omega

20

AILITH

Death was a giant, dwarfing even Fane. He was shrouded in black robes soaked with blood that left a swath of gore behind him as he advanced on his victims. He didn't seem to notice us as he passed, intent as he was on the crowd at the far end. The fetid odor of decay hung over him like a miasma, causing Grace to gag. She was no longer wearing a mask. None of us were.

The faces of the crowd were likewise bare, and we finally got a look at our companions. Aside for the horrified gape of their mouths, they looked…normal. Men and women who wouldn't have looked out of place buying from my market stall before the war or trading in Goldnesse in the aftermath. Just ordinary people.

How did they end up here, in such extraordinary circumstances?
From the crowd rose a strong voice. "Who dares? Who

dares insult us with blasphemous mockery? Seize him and unmask him, that…that— Shit." There was the quiet rustling of what sounded like paper and the clearing of a throat. "That we may know whom we have to hang, at sunrise, from the battlements!"

With a throat-rending battle cry, a figure broke away from the group and charged toward Death, waving the long, shining dagger. *William.*

He made it to only a few feet away from Death before the specter raised its hand. Blood poured first from William's eyes, nose, and ears, then from what seemed like every pore on his body.

It's not real. It's not real.

William collapsed on the floor, writhing in a pool of his own blood, and not a small amount of Death's. Death swept past him and headed for the keening horde. Some of them fainted outright, while others climbed over their companions as though trying to scale the walls to safety. William lay still, a heap of sodden rags against the dark floor.

As soon as he was out of Death's line of sight, he raised himself onto his elbow, and gestured to us, making a stabbing motion and pointing to Death's retreating back. Yards from the crowd, Death raised his hands again. Those closest to him began to bleed profusely, those behind them scrambling to keep their footing on the now-slick floor.

We cowered behind our pillar, keeping out of sight. Or so we thought.

"I believe we have some new guests this evening," Death intoned, turning toward us.

"Fuuuuuuck," Oliver moaned under his breath. "All right, which one of us is going to shank him?" No one said a word as Death began to glide our way.

"Anyone? Let's not all be heroes, eh? One at a time."

Silence. "*Anybody?*"

"I'll do it," Fane said. "I *am* the most powerful one here." He smirked and raised an eyebrow at Oliver, trying to goad him.

Oliver held up his hands. "No argument here. Have at it, Terminator."

"What's a—"

"Fane, you may want to do it sooner rather than later. Seeing as how Death is almost here." I nudged him. "Oliver, give him the shiv."

Fane looked down at the stake in his hand. "Does it matter if I do it underhand or overhand?"

"Christ, Fane, just use the pointy end!" Oliver looked as though he was ready to snatch the oversized splinter from Fane's hand.

Death was nearly upon us.

Keeping the shiv hidden close to his side, Fane approached Death. The apparition raised its hands, and blood leaked from Fane's eyes. Blood he didn't have.

Something's not right. Fane can't bleed. I've got to stop him. "Fane!"

I was too late.

Fane drove the wooden stake into where Death's soft belly should've been. Silence descended over the crowd.

Death stood still for a moment then his hands crept over the protruding end as though in disbelief. He staggered forward, and the crowd shrieked as one, drawing back against the wall again.

They wasted their breath. Death toppled backward, hitting the midnight tiles with a very human-sounding smack. His legs convulsed, once, twice, and then he was still.

Death was dead.

The room froze in stunned silence. William stood up

from his deathbed and rushed over to a pillar on the right side of the dance floor as the partygoers recovered from their shock and erupted into wild cheers.

All at once, the crowd vanished, as did the room's sinister façade. We stood in a near-empty room, furnished with only a few worktables holding tools and various pieces of junk and some metal chairs that looked a lot more functional than comfortable. A plain, concrete-floored, magnolia-walled room.

On the floor where Death had fallen lay a body. A *human* body with Fane's shiv jutting out of one eye.

He had killed Death all right, but Death was a man.

I know little about Will's past. Even Ailith, with her ability, had difficulty understanding it. Large pieces of it were missing, and those that remained were…dark. I understood his affinity with machines when the human world had been such a dangerous and painful place for him. And it was more than affinity he had for those androids—it was true affection. For Antoni, for all of them—and they for him. Antoni, already highly sentient when we met him, was one of those whose awareness was amplified by Fane, and his love for Will increased exponentially, like a dam inside him had finally burst. This outpouring of feeling was a salve for many of Will's old wounds, and indeed, for many of ours.

—Cindra, Letter to Omega

21

AILITH

Cindra rushed over to the body and scanned it. She looked at us and shook her head. "He's definitely dead. Fane's stake went straight into his brain."

"But I stabbed him in the stomach," said Fane, his eyes wide. Had he ever killed anyone before?

"You stabbed *Death* in the stomach. Right where this man's head happened to be." Admiration tinged Oliver's voice.

"It wasn't real. *None of it was real.*" Grace was dazed, clutching at the wall for support.

"Grace, sit down," I commanded. "And put your head between your knees."

She obeyed. I stalked over to William, who was bracing himself over what looked like a computer console, his head hanging down. "You want to tell us exactly what the hell is going on?" I demanded.

"You saved us," he replied, his breathing labored. "You saved *me*." He looked at the corpse and grimaced. "He's been holding me captive here for five years. *Five years.*" He backed up until his back hit the wall then slid down it to sit on the floor. "Thank you."

"I don't understand. What was all this?"

"This was my living nightmare. That…man," he pointed a shaking finger, "has been forcing me to take part in his hideous reenactments for years. He wasn't so bad at the start. It was something he did for fun, to pass the time and stay connected to the world above us." He drew a shuddering breath. "But eventually, he just went…mad, I guess. The stories got stranger and bloodier— I can't believe it's finally over."

"What were all those people?" Pax asked. As William and I spoke, the others had joined us, taking their places on the floor in a half-circle. "How did you create them?"

Will gave him an exhausted smile. "They're holograms."

"But they felt so real."

"Ultrasonics," he replied.

"*Soundwaves?*" Pax looked duly impressed.

"Yep. Acoustic radiation pressure. It creates a hologram that looks and feels real."

"Can you show me—"

"Pax, let William catch his breath. I think we all have a lot of questions." I hated to rebuke Pax, but William looked like he might faint.

Pax grinned. "Sorry," he said to William.

William held up a hand. "Don't be. I'd be happy to show you how it works."

"But before that," I said, "tell us how you ended up here."

"Wait," he said. "You seem to know who I am, but I have no idea who you are."

"I'm Ailith, Pantheon Modern Cyborg Program Omega cyborg O-117-9791."

"Pantheon Modern? That means—"

"We're the other cyborgs from your generation."

"How did you find me?"

"I heard you."

"Heard me? That's impossible. Who are you *really*?" He started to scramble to his feet.

I stood swiftly and reached out to him as the others rose and stepped back to give him space. "No, William, wait. I don't mean *hear* in the literal sense. I'm connected to other cyborg's minds. It's my…ability. I can't *read* your thoughts," I added hastily, "but I see what you see and feel what you're feeling." *And sometimes I can see your past.* I would save that for later. No need to make him any warier of us than he already was.

"You're kidding," he said, incredulous.

"Nope. We all have different abilities. Surely you must have one too?"

"I—" William's eyes widened and he pushed past me toward Fane. "You're—you're an artilect, aren't you?" His face was refreshed and alight, as though the angel had found again the light of his God.

"I am." Fane was tense, his voice guarded. I wasn't surprised. The Cosmists had fetishized him in a way that violated the rights he would've had as a human.

William circled him. "You're remarkable," he said. His tone was gentle, respectful, with none of the idolization I'd heard from others, including Stella.

Fane must've heard it too. "Thank you," he said, standing taller.

Oliver rolled his eyes and gagged.

"How did you know?" I asked. "What Fane was?"

"It's my ability. I have an affinity with machines—I can scan them, diagnose technical issues…"

"Like me," Cindra said. "Only I do it with humans. I'm Cindra, by the way."

The others introduced themselves. When Grace held out her hand, Will barely touched it before dropping his hand back to his side.

"Full organic human, right?" he asked.

"Yes." Grace's face reddened again.

"Hmm." He dismissed her and turned back to us, raising his eyebrows. "Soon after my cyberization, I was told we'd been discovered. That the Artilect War was about to officially kick off, and I had to go into hiding. We were on our way somewhere, some compound, when something happened. I still don't know what. The next thing I knew, I'd ended up here. With *him*."

"Did you know that man?"

"No, not until I was here. He told me his name was Lars. Why? Who is he?"

"I don't know for sure. I…saw him through the mind of another cyborg. He was posing as a doctor, but both he and that cyborg worked for the government. But the cyborg, Nova, I saw him through, ended up in the bunker you were supposed to be in."

"My *bunker*? What do you mean?"

"They moved all of us to hiding places across the province then kept us asleep for five years. You should've been with us. With him, specifically." I pointed at Oliver. "They replaced you with someone else—the cyborg who used to work with Lars. Before Oliver went to sleep, he was tipped off that she was a threat to us."

"Five years? You were asleep for five *years*? And replaced me? What happened to her?" He seemed genuinely confused. If he'd known about the switch, he hid it well.

"It's a long story, never mind," Oliver said hastily. I wasn't surprised he didn't want to discuss the details. He'd killed Nova, William's usurper, in a fairly violent fashion. "Whoever was behind the threat must've brought you here to keep you out of the way."

"Five years. So the war *must* be long over," William said.

"Yes. It's been over for a while."

"But then, if it's over, why did no one come looking for me?"

"We didn't know you were here. And with all the secrecy, maybe your location got lost." It sounded lame even to my own ears. *Just tell him the truth. Why hesitate?*

"I kind of suspected that. What happened? Who won? Sorry, that's a stupid question. Obviously, the Cyborgists won, or you wouldn't be here. Shit. That's a relief. Now we can live out in the open."

"Nobody won, William." I still couldn't bring myself to tell him the greater truth.

"Call me Will. What do you mean, nobody won?"

"It's… Well, it's hard to explain."

"No, it's not," Oliver interrupted, exasperated. "The world got fucked. Nearly everyone is dead, there's no sun, and people are constantly trying to kill us."

William's confused smile shattered and fell.

"Oliver!" Cindra admonished him.

"Sorry, but he's going to find out sooner or later. Seriously, you guys, he *knows* how long he's been down here."

"I can't believe the world is over." Will sank into the nearest chair, not bothering to move the jumble of wires and circuits. "The one comfort I had every night was the thought that even though I'd been forgotten, life had carried on above me." He stared off into the distance, his eyes unfocused. "Shit."

"Will, I'm so sorry. It was a shock for us too. Did you have any family?" I asked.

He ignored the question. "And you're the only cyborgs left? They told me others had survived. Only a few, but still. I wasn't the only one."

"There *were*."

"What happened to them?" From his downcast expression, he'd already guessed.

"That's also a long story," Oliver said. "And we'll be happy to tell you. But first, other than those freakish recreations, what have you been doing all this time?"

"I— Just living, I guess. Tinkering. Thinking. Waiting for this day."

"You were thinking about the others when I was inside your mind," I said. "What others? Who else is here?"

"The others are why Lars kept me alive. I'm their caretaker. To be honest, when you first called my name, I thought you were one of them, finally waking up…"

"One of who?" I prompted him.

He shook himself and stood up, gesturing for us to follow. "I'll show you. Not that they *do* anything. I'm not even sure they're alive. They didn't come with an instruction manual." As he spoke, he led us down another hall to a large chamber. Even before he turned on the lights, I recognized it.

Inside were row upon row of the dull metal cylinders. Now in the lit room, I saw them for what they were.

Each of the human-sized windowed metal pods were

inhabited, the still faces of young men and women visible through the panes, resting in an unconsciousness deeper than sleep.

"My God. There's *hundreds* of them." The columns of sleek pods filled the room, each one a host.

"One hundred and ninety-five," Will said.

"Who are they?" Cindra whispered, as though not to disturb them.

"Well," Will replied, "I guess you could say they're us."

I regret not being able to tell you more about the others of our kind, the ones we lost. My time with many of them was short, and in some cases, fraught with issues that may prejudice my judgment against the people they actually were or could've become. But you must remember their names and their existence. For they played a role, were part of the fine balance, and all our lives may have turned out differently without them:

Eire
Ella
Adrian
Ros
Cayde
Nova

—Cindra, Letter to Omega

22

AILITH

"What do you mean?" I examined their faces, searching for my doppelgänger. I was less surprised than I should've been.

"Oh. Not literally." He smiled in apology. "I mean, they're earlier versions of us."

The previous generations. *You are the fourth,* Mil and Lexa had said. Why were they here? Were they alive? How could they be? I ran my hand over the cold metal of a pod holding a woman with close-cropped black hair. Her face looked strangely taut, as though she found no rest even in sleep.

"How are these pods so cold?" I asked. The smooth surface was so chilled I couldn't touch it for more than a few seconds before my skin started to burn.

William pulled his sleeve down over his hand and ran it over the adjacent pod. "Cold water hydro runs through here. Also gives us our electricity."

I nodded. "That's common these days."

"Really? I just… I still can't believe it." He bent over and pressed his forehead against the freezing steel.

I had to turn away from his grief. I leaned over the pod again, wiping the pane with my sleeve. She was young, like us. They all were. Her face and what I could see of her body looked completely normal, no sign of trauma. "What happened to them?"

Will rubbed the red freezer burn on his forehead. "I don't know. They were here when I arrived. Lars told me to watch over them, to make sure they didn't wake up. He showed me how to use all the rudimentary controls, but beyond that, he wasn't particularly interested in answering my questions. I assume whoever chose me did so because of my ability."

"And you're sure you know nothing about Nova?" Oliver blurted. "I'm sorry, I just don't understand. If the Cyborgists put you here, they *knew* you wouldn't be with me. Mil and Lexa said they were surprised when we told them."

"They said a lot of things," I reminded him.

"Lexa? Middle-aged? Blond hair? Twisted her hands together a lot?"

"That sounds like her."

"I met her once, before I was brought here. But she didn't say anything about a bunker, or about these poor bastards here," Will replied.

My head was beginning to hurt. "Look, let's try to unravel the whole sordid story later." I turned back toward the pods. "So you don't know if they're alive?"

"They must be," Oliver said. "If they're dead, why haven't they decomposed?"

"Maybe it's too cold," William offered. "They've been like that the entire time."

"Ailith? Cindra? Can't either of you tell? Pax?"

Pax shook his head and retreated to the far side of the room. *That's not a good sign.*

I searched for their threads as Cindra used her ability to scan them. She frowned. "I can't seem to read anything through the metal. Ailith?"

Their threads were there, but faint. The light in them strobed in a strange way, different to anything I'd ever seen. In cyborgs, they burned steady, wavering when there were complications. In machines, they flickered. "Yes… It seems like they're there. But it's weird. Don't ask me to explain," I added as Fane opened his mouth. "Can we open one of the pods?"

Will put his hand protectively over the lid of the casing. "What if the pods are keeping them preserved? What if they crumble into dust? I'm supposed to be taking care of them."

"Well, then they're dead, and it doesn't matter, does it?" Oliver pointed out.

Will considered for a moment then nodded and stepped to the foot of the cylinder.

"Should I open all of them? Or just one?"

I looked at Cindra and shrugged. "All of them, I guess. It might be quicker to see if any of them are alive that way."

Will walked over to a panel set into the wall near the door. "I just have to line the command up…unlock this…open *this*, and—"

The lids unsealed with a faint hiss, lifting slightly. Will grabbed the rim of the closest pod and pushed it all the way open. A sweet smell, like rotten fruit on a warm day, rose from the exposed cavity.

A moment later, it hit me. One hundred and ninety-five threads flared, blinding me in both eyes. "Cindra, quick, they're alive!"

Screaming, pain, fear, and madness enveloped me in a chorus of one hundred and ninety-five voices. *Make it stop. Help us. Make it stop. Please. MAKE IT STOP.*

"Shut it!" Fane shouted from far away just as I could no longer bear it.

It stopped. I collapsed on the ground, still in darkness. Fane's hands gripped my shoulders, and his voice disturbed the air in front of my face.

"Ailith? Are you okay? Can you hear me?"

Reaching up to touch his face was the best I could do.

"What happened, Cindra? Are they alive?" His face turned under my fingers.

"According to my ability, they're dead. Their bodies anyway. Their brains are still alive somehow."

"It must be the pods." Fane's face turned back to me. "Ailith? What did you see?"

His face became a shadow then a form. "It was awful." My shoulders shook under his hands. "They… It was like they were in hell. They're in agony, and they're…trapped. But they *know* they're trapped. They're aware. But not."

Everyone was silent. I tried to think of a better way to explain. I couldn't.

"Have they been that way the whole time?" Will asked.

"I think so…" I tried to describe it without touching

my memory. I couldn't do it a second time. "Their minds are so broken, they don't understand the passage of time. So they live in the same excruciating seconds over and over."

Will shuddered, looking distressed. "I had no idea. I did honestly think they were gone. Is there anything we can do to help them?"

"Cindra?"

Her face swam into view, stark against her dark hair. "No. Their bodies have been dead for years. The pods are preserving them."

"We can't leave them like this. We have to help them." How many years had they been like that? *I can't. We have to do something.*

"A, the only—"

"Don't say it, Oliver."

"Fine, but you know as well as I do it's the only option."

I did know. "Will," I began, "if their bodies are dead, there's very little we can do to help them. Right, Cindra?" I desperately hoped she was going to have a better answer. She shook her head, so I continued. "I think the only thing we can do is—"

"Pull the plug?" Will asked.

"Yes."

He nodded once, his face calm.

"I thought you'd be upset." I didn't know what else to say.

"I am—because of what they're going through. Nobody deserves to live like that." He released a long, ragged breath. "To be honest, I was starting to think about topping myself before you came, and I'm fine, compared to them. *I* wouldn't want to live like that. If those pods are keeping them alive, like that, then when does it end for them? If I'd known—"

"You're going to *kill* them?" Grace's voice was shrill.

"Grace—"

"But they're *people*." She searched each of our faces, as though she would find a way to understand.

"This is what it means to be us, Grace," I said, more sharply than I'd intended.

Her eyes filled with tears, and she backed away from us. I'd seen the look in her eyes many times before. *Monsters. You're all monsters.*

And maybe we were. But we weren't the worst. These shells of our kin proved that.

"Are you okay, Will? Do you need a few minutes?" After all, he'd watched over them for half a decade.

"No, let's do it. Quickly, please," Will said. "They need this to be over, and so do I." He leaned over and pressed his lips to the window of the closest pod. "*Sueña con los angelitos*," he whispered. *Sleep with the angels.*

We shut down the main power supply and waited in silence.

"Why didn't you leave, Will? Was it just because of them?"

"That, and the fact that I can't. I'm not proud of it, but about three years ago, I did try. It's this stupid collar I ,ars put on me." He gestured to the thin metal band.

"I may be able to help you with that," Oliver said.

"Really?" Will asked, relief evident on his face. "Thank you. I don't think I could stay down here. Not if they're gone. And not knowing what I know now."

"If Oliver can help you, will you come with us?" I asked. "You would be more than welcome."

He smiled, the light returning to his face. "Yes, please. If I can. I've still got rations and some other stuff you might find useful—" He stopped. "Although…"

I waited for him to finish.

"No," he said, more to himself than me. "Don't."

I didn't pry. After a minute or so, he looked back at me, like he'd forgotten what he was doing.

I brushed my fingers over his shoulder. "Go gather everything you need. I don't want to rush you, but we're a bit short on time. I'll stay with them."

"What should we do about…Lars?" Oliver asked.

"Leave him, I guess." I still wasn't sure how to feel about what we'd done.

Fane stayed with me. We sat on the cold floor, side by side.

"Why do you think they put them here, Fane? Lexa said they were dead. And I mean they are, but not really. I don't understand why they kept them…alive, like that." For a moment, my vision blurred around the edges and a past ghost of Lexa bent over to kiss one of them briefly before closing the lid. The hand she laid on the window shook, and tears slid over the surface of the glass, marring the view. "Well, whatever the reason, I think she did care. In her own way." I leaned my head on his shoulder. "Are you okay?"

"Yes, why?"

"You killed someone, Fane. Was it the first time?"

"Yes."

"Do you not feel…upset?"

He seemed to consider it for a moment. "No. I think he was a very real threat to us. And what he was doing to those holograms—"

But they're just holograms, they can't feel anything, I wanted to say. But I didn't. How did I know they couldn't? And besides, did it matter? Lars was clearly unhinged. Why had he been left down here for so long? Had his superior died? Or had they intended to entomb him forever? I tried to stand, but my legs had gone numb from the cold floor.

"Do you think it's been long enough?" Fane asked as he helped me to my feet.

"There's only one way to know." I braced myself for an onslaught as we lifted the lid. There was nothing but silence this time; they were truly gone. Every single one of their threads had gone dark. We opened each of the pods in turn, just to make sure, and I felt not a whisper. We left the pod-room and went to find the others. Fane put his arm around me, helping to ease the emptiness in my chest.

"Is it done?" Will asked.

We nodded.

"You won't believe some of the stuff Will has," Pax said, his face flushed with excitement and his hands full of mysterious gadgets. "Show them, Will."

Will grinned shyly. "Well, I've had lots of time to work on stuff. I mean, I had to keep busy or go crazy like Lars." His smile fell a bit as he glanced toward the room that had held our predecessors. "Those holograms were something I was working on before the war. Whoever left me here left my stuff with me as well." He cradled a small black box.

"Watch this." Pax held his breath in anticipation, exhaling eagerly as a young man shimmered into existence before us. Taller than Will, slim, with dark hair, he stood smiling at us.

It was remarkable. I'd seen holograms before, loads of them, but nothing like this one. We circled him. How was it possible? He looked so real. Normally, holograms had a translucent appearance, a sort of ethereal aspect, but the man before us looked as corporeal as the rest of us.

"Can I touch him?" I asked.

Will nodded. "Of course."

I reached out and placed my hand on the young man's arm. He was warm to the touch, his skin soft and covered with tiny down hairs, just like a real person.

"He's incredible," Cindra said. I had to agree.

"Who is he, Will?" There was so much attention to the man's details that it had to be someone Will had known.

"He's… He died before the war." His voice was wistful as he switched the hologram off and packed it into a small case that he held to his chest. "I kept him secret for months until I got so lonely I couldn't stand it anymore. When I thought Lars was asleep, I activated him." His brow creased at the memory. "Of course, Lars caught me. He forced me to show him how I did it then used it to create scenarios like that monstrosity you witnessed earlier."

"Is this his?" Cindra asked, pointing to a worn notebook on one of the tables.

"Yes. Well, mostly. It's his diary. I took it over when he went properly over the edge. I figured we might both be dead by the time anyone found us, so I wanted to record what happened. Just in case we died doing something *really* weird." Will regarded the diary with distaste.

"Do you mind if I take it with me?" Cindra asked.

"No, not at all. Do you collect them? Seems a bit macabre."

"Something like that," she replied, tucking the book into her satchel.

We gathered what rations and tools Will had then filed into the pod-chamber for a last goodbye. *What will happen to them when we're gone?*

"Do you think they'll be okay?" Will asked, echoing my thoughts.

"I think so. I mean, they're at rest now."

He nodded, but his face still looked troubled.

"Now what?" Oliver asked.

"What do you mean? We go get Tor. And keep looking for allies," I said.

"Will should go back to the island. We can't expect him

to come with us where we're going. Not after everything he's already been through. Let the man live just a little bit longer, eh?"

"Where *are* you going?" Will asked.

We explained to him what had happened during our time at the compound and in Goldnesse, about Tor and the Cosmists. About our plan to save Tor and search for allies to help us when the Cosmists came for us.

Will gave a low whistle. "I missed all that?"

"Oh, don't worry, mate." Oliver laughed. "There's plenty more coming our way."

"And you need allies?"

"Why? You got some here?" Oliver peered under one of the pods.

"Not here… And it may be a long shot. Fane and Oliver might be able to make it work, but we'll have to go to them." Excitement crept into his voice, mingled with longing.

"Who is *them?*" I asked.

"How you feel about gynoids?"

23

AILITH

As we made our way through Richmond toward the massive industrial park, I bided my time fretting about the detour. Knowing that Tor was okay for the moment was the only thing that made it bearable. And if Will was right, and we gained some new allies, it would be worth it.

But gynoids? I didn't understand the connection. Gynoids were a specific type of android. Built to exceptionally high specifications, their quality was unparalleled by most androids. They looked, felt, and acted like real humans, but being machines, had no rights. Subsequently, they tended to be retained as companions for the very wealthy, or as sex workers for those with enough money to satisfy specific tastes. I'd seen gynoids up close only once, when I'd been a passenger in Adrian, another long-dead cyborg in our cluster.

Will explained as we traveled. "I used to work with them, the gynoids. Except," he added, "we called them androids, and if we find them, I ask you all to do the same. It might not seem like an important distinction to you, but it is. Anyway, I trained them in the nuances of human behavior, what customers would expect from them and how to react."

"So what happened to them?"

"Well, they're incredibly expensive, so when all this trouble started, we moved them out here to a nondescript warehouse and deactivated them."

"I still can't believe we're doing this," Oliver protested. "Even if we can get them to work, who's to say how they're going to react? What if they turn on us? Or what if they're useless? How are they going to help us? I don't mean to be crass, but considering what they were used for—"

"Are they self-actualized, Will? Like Fane?" I wanted to change the subject before Oliver gave himself an aneurysm.

Will considered. "Not exactly, but… I don't know how to explain it. They're not *supposed* to be, but there were times… I mean, you're the culmination of a process, right, Fane? There were others before you, less advanced but with the same qualities. Did you ever wonder where your precursors went? The ones that didn't quite make the grade? They would've been too costly to throw away, and what other industry aside from the sex trade or private collectors could afford such expensive units? While you were being feted, those who came before you earned their keep on their knees."

Fane looked appalled. "I never—"

"It's not your fault, Fane," I said. "And that's not what Will was insinuating, was it, Will?"

Will glanced between Fane and me, and his eyes narrowed. His mouth curved into a slight smile. "No. But is something you should be aware of. Or were you happier thinking they'd just been destroyed?"

"Will," I warned.

He surrendered, his hands in the air. "I'm sorry, Fane. I know you weren't responsible for any of it, but—"

"I understand," Fane replied. "And thank you for telling me. I didn't know, but I should have. I'm still learning."

"Welcome to being human," Will replied and clapped him on the shoulder.

"What did you teach them?" Grace was trying to be brave and having Will—another newcomer—with us seemed to have bolstered her confidence.

Cindra leaned over and whispered in her ear.

She blushed furiously and ducked her head.

Will laughed.

We finally entered the sect we'd been looking for. Like many of the others we'd passed, it was destroyed, the buildings obliterated under waves of bombs then picked over by survivors. Before the war, this area had housed a number of technology companies and would've been a prime target for the Terrans.

The building Will led us to hadn't escaped the blitz, and now appeared to consist mainly of a smashed foundation and twisted heaps of black-stained glass, concrete, and steel.

"Are you sure this is the right place? Aside from the fact it's clearly been looted, it looks like an office building." Oliver sounded relieved.

Will grinned. "They're underground."

"That seems to be a common theme with us," Oliver muttered.

It took Will several minutes to get his bearings. In the

far corner, he instructed us to lift away the debris, and there, under a pair of massive, warped steel doors and a mountain of smashed tile and melted carpet was a hatch.

"Everybody ready?" Will asked. He took a deep breath and wiped his hands on his trousers. He was so keyed up, he scraped his hip on the edge of the entrance as he stepped down into it.

At the bottom of the stairs, Will fiddled with the numbers on a manual lock before opening the door into a cavern-like room. One half of the room looked like a workshop, inlaid with long tables laden with diagrams and various tools. Others held limbs and molds, and still others various props of the androids' trade.

The other half of the room was empty of equipment. Instead, it was filled with rows of androids standing in formation, clothed in silk robes of all colors, like a field of wildflowers.

There seemed to be an android for every element in the human spectrum. Some were lush with exaggerated figures, others austere in their androgyny. Their ages ranged from a pair of just-legal twins to a silvered-haired matriarch with a stern countenance, and their skin, eyes, and hair flaunted every natural hue on the planet, and some that were decidedly otherworldly.

These perfect versions of humanity stood, their open eyes blank and unseeing, their hands loose at their sides. My eye was caught by a young female in sea-foam green, an abundance of red hair curling over one shoulder. I stepped forward to get a closer look.

You are very handsome. Adrian's android.

Behind her was the man from the hologram. Will had gotten every detail correct; it was a perfect likeness. Will noticed my interest and went up to him, running his fingertips down the side of the man's face. "Antoni. He's beautiful, isn't he? This android is the love of my life." He said it low so that only I heard. "I know you understand."

Did I? Before I'd met Fane, I would've felt very conflicted at the thought of being romantically involved with a machine. Before the war, it would've been considered taboo—and yet, only if the relationship was reciprocal. It had been accepted, if somewhat salacious, to frequent android brothels or have a companion, but an emotional attachment? Well, that gave the androids a humanity that was considered offensive by many. Enough to go to war over, at least.

"I do," I replied, and my heart swelled for this man I'd only just met.

"This is why I constructed the holograms. I thought if I could create some kind of replacement for them…they wouldn't be used for this purpose anymore."

"But then wouldn't they just dispose of the androids?"

He bit his lip. "Maybe. But I was hoping to patent the holograms and make enough money that I could buy them all the moment they were rejected. It sounds stupid when I say it out loud, doesn't it?"

"No," I replied. "I understand." And I did, although wasn't it merely trading one AI for another? Could holograms achieve sentience? It made my head ache.

Will turned back to Fane and the others and spread his arms wide. Each of them stared, absorbing what they saw in their own way.

"Welcome to my garden," Will said, bowing. "Each one a perfect and delicate flower. We got them from the Novus corporation then re-skinned them according to the market." He walked among the rows, touching this one's hand and that one's hair, his touch reverent. "I loved each of them. They were the reason I wanted to become a cyborg—to share a kinship with them, be closer to them. I always felt more comfortable with them than humans." He ran a hand through his ragged hair and smiled. "And of course, I wanted always to look this beautiful."

Fane watched him intently, his head tilted to one side.

"Are they—?" I asked

"Deactivated only. We never submitted the paperwork to have them decommissioned. When the Terrans began their little witch hunt, we brought them here and used a bunch of spare parts and greased palms to make it look like they'd been disposed of. It was one of the few things that gave me peace when I was underground, you know, thinking of them here, safe while the war raged around them. I thought perhaps one day, when things had gotten better, they'd be discovered and cherished as the treasures they are."

"That day is here, Will," Cindra said, putting her hand on his shoulder. "And I can't wait to meet them."

"Me neither," said Pax, curiosity and delight illuminating his face. "I'd hoped we'd get to travel down this timeline."

Will seemed to relax then, releasing a tension I hadn't detected. His smile was wide as he took in the room with a wave of his hand. "You want allies? My friends here may be your best shot."

"Look, I hate to be that guy—" Oliver began again.

"Then don't, love," Cindra said, her voice steely under her sweet tone.

Oliver gave up, shaking his head and leaning back against the wall.

"Satisfying yourself that you can rub it in when it all goes wrong?" I asked, trying not to smirk.

"What other choice have I got? But you can damn well bet that I will." He crossed his arms over his chest. "Well, let's get on with it, then."

Will rubbed his hands together. "I…I never thought I would see this day," he said. "I mean, I *hoped*, but…" He ran his hands through his hair then rubbed them together again. "Okay. Now the only thing we need to do is figure out how to activate them."

24

AILITH

Oliver was incredulous. "You mean you don't know how to activate them? I thought you were the one who *deactivated* them."

"No, I was just here for support."

"Oh, for fuck's sake." Oliver dropped his head into his hands and slid down the wall.

"I know *how* it was done, for the most part. There was an interface that connected to each of their brains simultaneously, and a signal was sent through to all of them at once."

"Okay, well that's a start." Oliver clambered to his feet. "So where's the interface?"

"Oh. Well, my boss took it with her. But I thought you

were some sort of human computer." Will smiled sheepishly.

"I am, but I can't connect to them if they're not active."

Will's chest heaved as though he was going to throw up.

"Ailith can do it," Fane said.

"What? No, I can't. I have no idea how to activate them."

"You can see their threads, right? The threads connecting you to them?"

"Technically, yes. I mean, I can *see* threads, but because they look like every other machine's, I'm not entirely sure which ones are theirs. Even if we can figure out how to send the signal, we might wake up God-knows-what." *The mech in the forest, it's skeletal driver still at the controls.* I shuddered.

"The code to activate them should be unique, shouldn't it?" Fane looked at Will, who nodded in confirmation.

"Yeah. We deactivated them before that all-purpose government pulse was sent. Standard machines were required to have a basic code that allowed them to be deactivated if necessary. It was one of the conditions companies had to adhere to be legal." He grinned. "But these aren't standard machines, and my boss was never one to let others make her decisions for her."

"Okay, so how do we access the code?" I asked.

"I have it on a chip," Will said.

"Please, tell me you have it with you?" Oliver said. I had no doubt even the nanites wouldn't be able to stop him getting gray hairs after today. *When did you start worrying about anything, Oliver?*

"Of course I do," Will said, looking offended. "It's here." He held out his forearm. "It was embedded in my arm for safekeeping."

"Okay, that I can work with," Oliver said. "I'll read the

code from you then give it to Ailith so she can do her mind-meld trick."

The code entered my awareness only a few minutes later. I closed my eyes and readied myself to send the code out and revive ninety-nine of the dark threads in my network.

Nothing happened. All around me, the intensity of certain threads increased then faded, like a failing heart.

"Fane, I need to you to help me. I don't have enough power to do it on my own."

"Sure you do, A," Oliver said. "Flick the switch. It'll work for androids as well as cyborgs."

The switch was something he'd put inside me months ago.

The original intent for your ability would've allowed you to be present in every connected cyborg simultaneously… I can't guarantee that your mind would be able to process it fast enough. I don't think they expected you to live very long.

"No way, Oliver. We don't know what will happen, or if I'll even be able to switch it off. The situation's not that dire—yet. Fane?"

Fane stood behind me and pressed as much of his body against mine as possible.

"You know you don't have to do that for it to work, right?" I asked him.

"I know," he said, his smile tickling my scalp. "But it's a lot nicer like this."

I couldn't disagree.

I gathered the pulse of code in my mind again, focusing the energy on the threads that had flashed before. Fane's energy blended with mine, and my power increased tenfold. In a sudden burst of light, I connected with each of them and sent the code hurtling into their brains, along with a silent prayer.

In front of us, where ninety-nine glorified dolls had stood, ninety-nine androids blinked.

25

AILITH

Some of the androids fell to their knees. Others touched their faces, running their fingertips over their lips and throats. Even more remained stoic, unmoving, as though waiting for a command. Antoni, the man from the hologram, rushed to William, his face softening into a more than human expression as they embraced each other.

After his reunion with Antoni, Will briefly checked each of the androids, asking them questions and listening intently to their answers. I approached him just as he was finishing with the last one, the silver-haired matriarch. She eyed me haughtily, her eyes narrowed. Then, she seemed to realize what I was, and her expression tempered.

"How are they?" I asked.

126

"In remarkably good condition," he replied. "Of course, no time has passed for them. They may be a bit stiff at first, like any machine or person would be, but they're pretty much the way I left them years ago."

"So what do we do now?"

"I'll explain everything that's happened to them. Then, I'll introduce you all and your situation. Then…well, we'll have to see. I don't know that they have a program to accommodate these circumstances. They'll be acting on their own. I won't force them to choose you."

The androids listened to Will's story with very human expressions of bewilderment as he explained about the war, the change in their situation. That they were no longer pets or servants, that their bodies and awarenesses were now their own. I could empathize; I still remembered the moment Tor told me that everything I'd known was gone.

"What do you mean by *free*? Where will we go? What will we do?" Their voices all chimed in at once.

Will explained who and what we were. The androids looked at us with curiosity. Just how sentient were they? Were we as extraordinary to them as they were to us? Did they think it eerie how much *we* looked like *them*?

Will gave them a condensed version of our story and our needs. He described what had happened in Goldnesse, about Ethan and the inevitable confrontation to retrieve Fane, and about our subsequent need for allies on our island.

"Are we to be your shield?" one of them asked. There was no accusation or discontent in his voice, merely the curiosity of duty.

"No! Of course not," I replied hastily. "You don't *have* to come with us, and even if you do, you don't have to fight or defend us. It's not your fight. Come or not, fight or not, it's your choice."

He seemed to turn this information over in his mind. "Why does this Ethan want...him?" He tilted his head toward Fane but didn't look at him. Will had left out some details for the sake of summarizing our journey.

"He wants to create more artilects, fully sentient ones like Fane. But most of his records were destroyed, so he needs Fane's brain to fill in the gaps. Fane does not wish to comply."

"Did Ethan create this Fane?"

"Yes. He created all of you. He was the head of Novus Corporation."

The android lifted his leg and peered at the bottom of his foot. Stamped into the flesh was the Novus Corporation symbol. *That* name they knew. "They created us," he echoed.

"Then they threw us away," another one said. "Because we were not like *him*." Ninety-nine pairs of eyes turned toward Fane, and I was surprised at the hostility in them. "And now they want to destroy him?" Her voice held no mercy.

"Not exactly," I said. "They only want to create more artilects. But it *could* destroy him, and he's one of us now, so they can't have him." I reached out and squeezed his hand. He smiled at me. The exchange wasn't lost on the androids.

"That wasn't the only reason I left them." Fane addressed the androids, though most of them wouldn't meet his gaze. "I may be closer to their idea of perfection than you, but I still had no rights. They didn't see me any differently than they saw you. It may have been only a matter of time before I was auctioned off and joined you."

The thought of Fane living as these androids had made me sick to my stomach.

"And now, they're trying to kill my friends, simply

because they want their property back. They don't value the life that they gave me, other than as a testament to their skill. They don't value any real life. That's why they're holding our friend Tor hostage. Even now, they're still using androids like you. They have an AI with them called Umbra. She killed a friend of ours, and she wants to take this one's body." He nodded at me.

Oliver snorted. "God, this sounds like the worst soap opera ever."

"What would we do in this place?" the first android asked as the rest of them drew closer to us. It appeared he was closer to Fane's level of sophistication than some of the others, who seemed content just to listen impassively.

"Whatever you want. Fish, learn to draw, plant a garden." My answer was met with some consternation and a little alarm. *I shouldn't be surprised. Why wouldn't they find it a strange concept?*

"What if we break down?" Another one, a tall, exotic-looking woman, asked.

Oliver stepped in. "We have some equipment back on the island, and we're planning to gather more. In fact, if you do decide to join us, that's what you can do on your way back. I'm sure Will knows where to shop."

Will nodded. "In fact, a lot of the stuff we'd need is right here. Between all of us, we can easily carry it back—we'll just have to improvise." He didn't let go of Antoni's hand as he faced the androids. "Well? What do you all think? Do you want to go? With them?"

None replied.

"Do you want us to give you some privacy?" I asked.

Will considered the androids then nodded. "I think so. Thank you."

We crowded into the stairwell and shut the door behind us. Low murmurs followed, but I couldn't make out what they were saying.

After a few minutes, Will opened the door and ushered us back in. The androids had grouped closer together, their eyes trained on us.

"We've decided to come with you," Will said. "All of us."

"I'm glad to hear it." And I was. More than glad. Having them with us could make the difference in our survival—and theirs.

"Would any of you be willing to come with us on this suicide mission?" Oliver asked.

Will looked uneasy. "I—"

"They can't," I interrupted.

"Why not?" Oliver was confused. "We need all the help we can get."

"Because. It's not their fight. Not yet, anyway," I replied. "But more than that, what if Ethan or, God forbid, the Saints, get their hands on any of them? Who knows what they'll do to them? Or with them? Or what if Ethan has some way to control them—"

Oliver held up a hand. "I get it. Ugh. You're right. It's better we keep them a secret for as long as we can."

Will's relief was palpable. The android's expressions were neutral.

"So they're going back—which raises another question: who's going to take them?" Oliver asked.

Grace stiffened, her expression alarmed.

"Relax, Grace," I said. "If Pax says you should come, you're coming."

She pressed her hands to her cheeks and nodded. *I wonder how Tor would feel, knowing how devoted she is to him?* "I think Fane should go," I said. He looked at me, stricken. "Fane, you know what Will and the androids will need, and you know how to get back to the island. I think it's too dangerous for you. I'm sorry." The androids looked between Fane and me with interest. Would he obey my commands? Even with his freedom? Fully aware that everyone could hear, my words came out in a rush. "Fane, please. You're too important to me."

He pressed him mouth into a thin line. He didn't like it, but I'd hit him where it hurt. "Fine," he acquiesced reluctantly.

As Will answered the androids' questions and instructed them on which equipment to gather, Fane pulled me to one side. "I'll go back with them, but I'm not happy about it."

Gray clouds rolling over the horizon. A broken mirror.

"I know. But I think it's the best thing, Fane. I don't want to lose you as well."

He brushed his thumb over my cheek and smiled. "I can't complain about that. I don't want you to lose me either." He hesitated. "You've noticed that the androids don't like me, haven't you?"

I kissed the palm of his hand and smiled. "Don't worry, they will." Despite what I'd said, uneasiness unfurled in me. *They wouldn't hurt him, would they?* Surely once they spent some time with him, they'd accept him. Was I doing the right thing by asking him to go with them? Or was I putting him at risk? Fane was formidable, but against ninety-nine androids? He'd be impossibly overmatched.

"Don't worry, Ailith. They might not care for me, but they also have very little idea about the outside world. They need us as much as we need them. I can use that to my advantage. I'll be fine, I promise."

I hoped he was right.

***

We parted ways in the morning. Fane hugged me so

tightly I had to thump him on the back to get him to let me go. He looked over his shoulder as they walked away, his expression forlorn.

The androids gave him a wide berth, choosing to walk several yards behind him. I hoped his journey back wasn't going to be too unpleasant. Their disdain would bother him, I knew. Even though Fane was an artilect, he was sentient, and it was an innate part of his personality to be friendly and want people to like him. He was used to people treating him a particular way because of what he was, and, well, he was a little spoiled. True, both before and after the war, people had wanted to destroy beings like him, but he'd never been exposed to it personally. Instead, he'd been worshipped and adored.

He'd told me once that he didn't want to *be* human, but wanted to be treated like one. Well, he was about to get his wish.

Though, I suppose CIVRS did serve a purpose. Although it wasn't enough to force the government to slow down the progress of companies like Novus and Pantheon Modern, it did allow me to find someone like Nova. Someone broken enough to do what we wanted without implicating ourselves. Her, plus our guy in PM, and we were good to go. They were in such a rush to churn out those cyborgs before they got shut down they didn't even notice an extra one being slipped in.

—Lars Nilsson, personal diary

26
FANE

The androids didn't like me. They avoided me, and I couldn't blame them. They were created for the same purpose as I was, to be revered, but they'd been found wanting, their sentience not sentient enough. Then they weren't only discarded but sold to the highest bidder and degraded, and all because of Ethan's desire to be God.

How *sentient were they? Each seemed different, some more aware of their situation than others. Several of them spoke amongst themselves, while the rest seemed happy just to take one step then the next. It was disconcerting, and I finally understood how I must make people—and even the cyborgs—feel, and why our creation had been so alarming.*

They'd find them even more alarming now. Before, dressed in the silk robes so at odds with the outside world, they were defined as other, their purpose-built attributes emphasized. But in a strip mall that had survived the bombings, they'd found a store that specialized in selling merchandise to tourists. And although much of it had already been stripped by looters, all ninety-nine had managed to outfit themselves with far more practical clothing. Now, dressed in sweatshirts proudly claiming themselves as Canadian, they looked like a tour group winding down the coast to go orca-watching. The disappearance of their otherness, something the Terrans had long feared, was complete.

It had been all over Ryan's face.

I'd been walking almost on autopilot, lost in thought, when he'd stepped out in front of me from his hiding place along the path. The others were far enough behind me to be concealed by the trees, and he'd assumed I was alone.

"Fane."

It took me a second to bring my thoughts back to the present. "Ryan. Where did you come from?"

He pointed to a thick mass of brush. "There. I heard someone coming so I hid. Then I saw it was you."

"You've come for Grace?"

"Of course." His face darkened. "That means she found you. Where is she? We need to have a little chat then we're going home."

Water with no visible bottom. Dark shapes. *"She's not here."*

"What do you mean, she's not here? Where—" His eyes widened, and all color fled his face.

I didn't have to look behind me to know why.

"Ryan, meet our allies," I said quickly. His hand was halfway to the gun he kept slung over one shoulder.

"Our allies?"

"Yes. This is William. He's another one of the Patheon Modern cyborgs." William stepped forward.

"Another? I thought—"

"Don't worry, I'm the only other one." William gripped the hand that was still in midair and shook it briskly. Before Ryan could reply,

he added, "And these are my friends. And now they're your friends too."

Ryan smiled in response, a reflexive smile that didn't reach his eyes. "Nice to meet you. Fane, could we have a word in private, please?"

"Of course." I nodded to Will then Ryan and I continued ahead for several yards back the way he'd come.

Before I could reassure Ryan, he let loose on me. "What the hell is going on, Fane? Who are those people? And where is Grace?"

"They're not people, Ryan. Not the way you think. They're androids. Will used to work with them."

"Androids? And who's this Will? If he's one of the cyborgs, why didn't we know about him before? Did the others know about him?" Frustration roughened his voice; he must've been afraid. I wasn't surprised.

"They thought he was dead. On the way back to the compound, Ailith heard him with her ability. We found him locked in a bunker like the others were. Once he knew we were looking for allies, he took us to the androids." I didn't think mentioning the other nearly two-hundred now-dead cyborgs would help the situation.

"And we can trust them?"

"I think so. I mean, we do have a common enemy in Ethan. His company, the Novus Corporation, built them. And then threw them away. We gave them the option to come with us, no strings attached, and every last one chose to do so."

He didn't look convinced, peering over my shoulder, his lips pressed into a thin line.

"They don't dislike humans, if that's what you're worried about, although they have every right to. They just… They were given life and then told how to live it. And now that's changed. They have some adjusting to do, but none of that involves annihilating the human race."

He smiled humorlessly. "Well, there's only one of me, so who am I to argue? Besides, my primary concern is Grace. I'm glad you all decided to be sensible and turn back." His gaze searched beyond the androids. "So where is she?"

I didn't have a lot of experience with confrontation, and a new sensation flooded me.

A large crowd, no way out.

"Fane? Fane! I said, where is she?"

Inexperience made me blunt. "She's not here. They're still going to the compound, and Grace went with them."

Blood surged into his face. "What? They've taken Grace with them? You can't be serious." He took a step toward me, and his hand hovered over his rifle again.

"She insisted."

"She insisted? And you're telling me that an artilect and four cyborgs couldn't overrule the insistence of a sixteen-year-old girl?" His voice reached a crescendo that drew one hundred pairs of eyes. Aware he suddenly had an audience, he pulled me farther down the path.

"What's the real story, Fane? Now, I might not agree with everything—hell, most things—those cyborgs do, but I do know Cindra well enough to know she would never willingly put Grace at risk. So what's the truth?"

There was no way to say it that would make it sound good. "Pax said we needed her to retrieve Tor, that she was crucial to our success—"

"Which way did they go?" His face contorted into a feral snarl.

"Ryan, she'll—"

"Which way?" He grabbed the front of my coat, and his strength surprised me. Was it love for his child? Fear? Or was—

"Fane!" His whitened knuckles were inches from my face. He definitely wasn't thinking rationally.

"Sorry, Ryan. They've gone back along the original route." I pulled out my copy of the map and traced it for him. "But, they'll be fine. They won't let anything happen to—" My words were rendered useless by his retreating back. He pushed past Will and the androids, his fear of them neutralized by a greater one. As he disappeared among the trees, I wished I could send a message to Ailith. *Watch out.*

"Is everything okay?" Will asked. I hadn't heard him come up beside me.

"No, but I hope it will be."

"He seemed…nice," he said diplomatically.

"Grace is his daughter. And she snuck away to follow us."

"Ah. What did he think of his new allies?"

"About what you'd expect. He wasn't one of those who was against their creation, but he was a victim of it indirectly. He'd never admit it, but he was more afraid than anything."

"As long as it's not the kind of fear that turns violent," Will said. "I won't put them at risk again."

"It's not," I assured him. "He'll come around. And his wife is a good woman. She knew what the cyborgs were and kept their secret. When they were exposed by one of their own, Lily and Ryan did their best to protect them—at the cost of their home and the new life they'd built."

Will considered then lifted his chin. "Well, we owe them respect, if nothing else. Now what?"

"We keep going. The sooner we get everyone back to the island, the better."

Will nodded and returned to the androids. As we recommenced our journey, he took Antoni's hand.

Stop looking, Fane. But I couldn't. They seemed so happy, or at least Will did. Antoni seemed to be one of the more sentient androids, gazing at Will with an expression that, if not adoration, demonstrated a very definite connection.

Could it ever be the same for Ailith and me? Could she forget about my artificialness? The fact that I was mostly synthetic? So far, it didn't seem to matter, emotionally or physically, but what about a few years down the road? She was part machine, but surely she would age eventually. How long could the nanites keep rebuilding themselves and replenishing her? Would it make a difference? It wouldn't to me.

But to her?

And of course, there was the question of Tor. Could I compete with him? Was there even a competition? I wasn't jealous about their relationship, their closeness. It made me…sad. Petals torn by wind and rain. A house, abandoned too quickly. *They were the same.*

Later, as I led us across the water in the scores of rowboats we'd gathered, I turned my mind to other things. There was no point dwelling on what would happen in the future. Right now, we had to focus on making sure we had one.

We're so close. Tomorrow, we'll be at the compound, and I'll be able to see his face again. How will he react? I feel nervous now. What if too much has happened in the meantime? What if he thinks my leaving him behind was a betrayal? Hopefully, he'll see my sacrifice for what it is, and it will be enough for him.

—Love, Grace

27

AILITH

"Do you think we should have sent Grace back with the others? Ryan and Lily are going to kill us, *all* of us. You understand that, right?" I complained to Oliver as we hiked side-by-side. Cindra was deep in discussion with Pax about the twisted grass we'd found near Will's bunker.

"No, they won't. They'll understand. Why are you second-guessing it now?"

"Grace is their *child*, Oliver. Their *only* child. And she disappeared right as we were going on a journey. A journey Ryan thought was too dangerous to go on himself." I glanced over my shoulder to where Grace straggled behind us. She was having trouble keeping up but refused to let us stop and rest for her.

"Well, there's not much we can do about it now."

Oliver was right, but it was so irritating that I couldn't let it go. I was on edge about everything—Tor, Fane, *everything.* Oliver's nonchalance was simply the last straw. "There is. We can't get Grace involved."

"Pax says we have to," Oliver replied between his teeth. "Get over it."

We entered the small clearing where we'd found William. Cindra had just bent to retrieve a sample of the grass for her collection when a man spoke up from behind us.

"You don't care who you have to use to get your way, do you?"

Ryan. He must've tracked us from the island. He looked exhausted, his face lined with fatigue and anger. "I ran into Fane and your…allies. He told me the direction you were taking."

"Ryan—" I began.

"No. How dare you? Grace is only sixteen. I know she snuck away to join you, and I don't blame you for that. But the moment you discovered her, you should've turned around and brought her back. But then you only care about Tor, don't you?"

I'm not the only one.

Grace looked shocked, the color gone from her face. She was poised on the balls of her feet, almost like she was going to run. *Don't, Grace. You'll only make it worse.*

I couldn't meet Ryan's eyes. Even after everything I'd been through, I still felt the mortification of being chided by a parent.

"Grace, we are going back to the island, *now*. And then we're going to leave and find somewhere else to live. Somewhere where these…cyborgs aren't constantly putting us in danger."

Grace made her decision and stood her ground. "No, Dad. I *have* to go with them. Pax says I'm important. I have to go and—" She bit her lip.

"Pax said? *Pax said?* Pax can—"

"She's right, Ryan. We need her for this mission to be a success." Pax said it mildly but stared at Ryan with an unusual, and unnerving, intensity.

Once Ryan had gotten over his shock that the normally pleasant-mannered Pax had dared to contest him, he sputtered in indignation. "No, Absolutely not. It's *dangerous*, Grace. You saw what that mob was like when we left. If I'd thought it was in any way safe, we wouldn't have left in the first place!"

"Ryan." I put my hand on his arm, but he jerked it away. "We can't take any chances. If Pax says we need her, I believe him. I don't like this any more than you do. I don't *want* Grace to be involved. But if we don't succeed in getting Tor back, we don't know what's going to happen."

"I'm not putting my daughter at risk just so that you can save your boyfriend." His fists clenched convulsively at his sides, as though he was going to strike me.

"That's not what this is about, Ryan. How would you feel if it was Grace being held captive by Ethan? Would you tell us to just leave her there?"

He closed his eyes. "No," he said, "of course not. But—"

"Look, I promise we'll keep her out of harm's way. It's not like she needs to go *into* the compound or see anyone. We're going to find the entrance we used to escape the first time and enter the compound from there. And that entrance is over a mile away." I tried one last plea. "Come with us, Ryan. That way, you can make sure we don't involve her any more than necessary."

"We don't actually need Grace at all," Pax said.

"Wait, *what?*" I asked incredulously. "I thought Grace was crucial. You said—"

"She *was,*" he replied. "But it's actually Ryan we need.

Grace was just bait so that he'd follow us."

Ryan looked as confused as I felt. "Why didn't you just say that in the beginning? Ask me to come?"

"Would you have left Lily and Grace?" Pax pointed out.

"No, I probably wouldn't," Ryan admitted. "But if I'm as important as you say, Pax, that was a pretty risky gamble."

Pax smiled. "I have insider information."

Grace looked crestfallen. She'd wanted so badly to be important, to play a role rescuing the man she…loved?

Ryan sighed. "The answer is still no. I won't put Grace at risk. I'm sorry, but you'll have to find a way to rescue Tor without us."

"Grace will be fine, I promise." Pax smiled his earnest smile.

I had to bite my tongue. Pax often left out crucial information for things to go the way he wanted. He didn't lie, exactly, just omitted. *I hope he's right about Grace being fine.* But, if Pax said it was the only way, I trusted him on that, at least.

"They're coming for us, Ryan. They have Umbra, weapons…we need all the help we can get, even with the androids."

Ryan looked at Grace as he turned over the options in his mind. "We'll compromise. I'll take Grace back to the island then come back—"

"No."

Ryan turned around.

Grace stood behind him, her feet planted firmly, her fingernails digging into the flesh of her hips. "I'm not going back."

"Grace—"

"No. You can't make me."

"Actually," Ryan said, "I can."

Grace glared at him. "If you do, I'll follow you. I'll wait until you're gone then I'll come after you."

"You—"

"Is that what you want? Me, on my own? Trying to find you?"

"Your mother will make you stay."

"She can't. She'll have to sleep sometime…and when she does—"

Ryan stared at his daughter, who only five years ago had been a child. He took in her whitened knuckles, her stony expression. "Grace, why does this mean so much to you?"

I waited for her to say it out loud.

"Dad, we have to do this together. Or it won't work. Pax said so." She made no mention of Tor. She probably knew that using true love as a reason would have her father marching her back to the island immediately.

"No, I'm sorry Grace, but there's nothing Pax could say that would make me put you in danger." He grabbed her arm and began to propel her back the way we'd come. This time, she didn't resist.

"I could tell you the truth." Pax stood tall, his gaze pinning Ryan where he stood.

For a moment, Ryan was taken aback. "The truth? The *truth* is that you—"

"He'll kill us all."

"Ethan? That's exactly why I don't want Grace anywhere near that compound."

"Tor."

"Tor? Pax, what are you talking about?" This information was new to me.

"I'm talking about time. If you take Grace home, Ryan, we will run out of time."

"Time for what?"

"We're at a crossroads. If we don't go now, if we don't

get Tor out when we're supposed to, the path changes. Ethan will adjust his plan. He'll warp Tor, the way he did Umbra. Tor will no longer be the bait—he'll become a weapon, as he was built to be. Tor and Umbra together."

A chill bloomed behind my eyes and curled down my throat to take root in my stomach. *No.* If that happened, I would have to choose between Tor and us. Neither option was one I could live with.

My distress must've drunk the color from my face because Ryan's hand fell from Grace's elbow.

"Ailith, is that true? Did you know?"

"Help me, please. Trust me." On the surface, Pax's face was impassive.

I hated lying, but— "It's true." Cindra looked sharply at me, but Oliver only rocked his head slightly in understanding. "We didn't want to alarm you, because we thought we would make it in time, but Pax is right. This isn't just about saving Tor—it's also about preventing Ethan from using him against us." My very bones were weary at the thought.

Ryan frowned. "Can't you control him? I thought that was one of your abilities."

"I don't know," I said, and that was true enough. I could get inside him, but anything beyond that was still up in the air. "Who knows what they've done to him? And even if I could, that's *all* I'd be able to do. And I don't know for how long. That's why it's so important we get him back."

Ryan searched Pax's face then mine, trying to ferret out our lie. We gazed steadily back at him, united.

"Is that true Pax, what you said about Tor? That he would kill us all?"

"No. But he would kill you."

That was good enough for me. "Ryan, please. Help us. We don't have much time, and the longer we stand here, the greater our risk." I looked pointedly up at the sky, which was just reaching the apex of its paleness.

Caught by indecision, Ryan paused. And that was enough. Grace sensed the chink in his armor and took her chance. "I promise to stay out of the way, Dad. I'll do everything you tell me. *Please*, just let me help."

He looked at Pax, his expression grave. "And you're sure about this, Pax? You need us? And Grace won't get hurt? I need you to be honest with me."

I held my breath.

Pax spoke the truth. "We need you, Ryan. And Grace will not get hurt at the compound. I promise."

Ryan bowed his head to kiss the top of Grace's, his face troubled. He exhaled into her hair then gripped her by the shoulders. "I don't like it, but it seems like we have little choice. But, Grace," he warned as her face lit up, "you have to do exactly what I tell you. Or we turn around immediately, Tor or no Tor."

Grace squealed and threw herself against her father's chest. Hugging her close, Ryan muttered, "Your mother is going to kill me." Then as Grace clung to him, he peered over her head at the rest of us. "So, what's the plan?"

It didn't take much to convince Nova to do it. We simply told her what she wanted to hear—how special she was, how she was going to change the world. Probably the only time in her life that she ever felt important. She was so desperate that she didn't even mind becoming one of them. Of course, she didn't know that the virus we planted in her would kill her as well. Suicide mission, and the dumb kid didn't even know.

—Lars Nilsson, personal diary

28

AILITH

"*Shit.* We should've expected this. When we escaped, Ethan and Lien obviously would've wanted to know *how.* Mil and Lexa were probably only too happy to oblige them."

The emergency tunnel we'd used to escape when Ethan and his followers had descended on the compound had been caved in by an explosion. Our secret route to the compound and Tor was completely and utterly blocked by the ruins of a small mountain.

"Now what do we do? Try to clear the debris? Try to bust our way through? We should've brought the bloody androids." Oliver had been crabby enough after another uncomfortable night on the ground. At the sight of the blocked tunnel, he'd sunk onto an errant boulder and dropped his head into his hands.

"Clearing that debris could take days," I said. "We have no idea how far back the collapse goes. I think we need a new plan. And there's a cactus on your foot."

Ryan looked around, shaking his head. "It's too quiet. Why are there no scouts? Why is no one waiting for us?"

"That means Ethan has a plan," Oliver replied, gingerly pulling the cactus away from his ankle. "Probably one which wants us in or much closer to the compound. It's still too risky for him to meet us out here, or he's feeling cocky. Either is a good sign for us."

"How?" Ryan asked. "They have the advantage now—they knew that if they cut off your route here you'd have to go in through the front door, which is suicide."

"Exactly." Oliver looked pleased.

"Since you look like the cat who got the canary, I assume you have an alternative plan?" I asked. "Care to share? Because right now, your face is so smug it had better be an amazing plan."

"It is. Remember the other false entrances?" he asked.

"Yes, but they don't lead *into* the compound, remember?"

"No, they don't. But I don't think that matters. I have the diagrams here, somewhere in my mind. Give me a few minutes." Oliver braced his hands on his knees, and his expression became distant.

"Maybe we could cause some kind of distraction? Draw them out. Maybe explosives?" Pax suggested hopefully.

"That's not a bad idea, but how do we make them? Everything we need to make bombs is either back on the island or in the compound storage room."

Ryan spoke up. "I can make explosives. You wouldn't believe how many homemade bombs I saw during my time on the force. All it takes is some household chemicals, the kind that most scavengers wouldn't be interested in.

There's a farm store a couple of miles from here." He pointed south. "I'll go see if I can find the chemicals we need. And I'll also look for some shovels and trowels, just in case Oliver's plan doesn't work out and we have no choice but to go digging."

As he finished speaking, Oliver came back to the present. "Okay, I have a plan that might work. Is there any way to get Tor out of wherever he is?"

"You mean rather than us going in?"

"Yes. I know we're superhuman and all, but we're no match for a bunch of guns. We heal quickly, but not *that* quickly." He raised an eyebrow at me. "So? Can you?"

"I don't see how. I've only controlled him a few times, and only for short periods. And it's not like I can just tell him where to go." We'd been given certain limitations to curb our amassed power, and that was mine. I could be in any of the other cyborg's minds, but aside from being able to speak to Pax, I had no agency, no way to communicate.

Or did I?

"Actually…I may be able to give him a message," I said slowly. "It's not a sure thing, though."

"None of this is," Oliver pointed out.

"Okay, so say I *can* get a message to Tor. What do I tell him? What's the big plan?"

"You know how the false entrances don't lead into the compound, but somewhere into the mountain, like a warren? One of them crosses almost directly underneath your garden. Close enough that we could go down that tunnel and dig up into your garden floor."

"That could work," I agreed. "But then what?"

Pax said, "In one of the futures, Tor is in the garden, waiting for us."

"Exactly," said Oliver. "They'd never suspect that. We could have him out of there and be halfway back to the island before they even realize he's gone." He looked at me. "What do you think, A? Could you get him to come down to the garden?"

I ran through the scenario in my mind. "I'm not sure…but I can try. I'll know if he understands or not. But then, of course, there are the issues of him being drugged *and* under guard. There's no way Ethan would leave him alone."

"Me, Cindra, Grace, and Ryan can distract them," Pax said. "With *explosives*." He looked thrilled at the idea. "When the bombs go off, they'll all come running."

"Yes, but the minute you start causing a distraction, Ethan will know we've arrived. The first think he'll do is try to lock Tor down." I had no doubt Ethan had instructed anyone watching Tor to take him down at the first sign of trouble.

"Well, hopefully we won't need the distraction. And if we do, Tor'll just have to figure it out." Oliver's mind was made up. "Give him the message now, before Ryan gets back, so he has time to come up with a plan to get to the garden. Let's hope he's as clever as he is devastatingly handsome," he quipped, "because this will be the only chance we get."

He's so incredibly creepy, that William. He looks completely human…but I know he's not. That was one of our main problems with them—if they'd somehow marked them…branded or tattooed them in some way, maybe people would've felt differently. We would've known what they were, and we could've treated them accordingly. But no, they wanted to hide them amongst us, allow cyborgs the same freedom as human citizens. Why, if not to eventually replace us one by one? Well, not down here. I've put a collar around William's neck. Sarah left it for me, and I wasn't going to use it, but he walks too quietly, speaks too politely. I bet he's just waiting for the right time to kill me. Well, the joke's on him. If he tries to leave or comes within arm's reach of me, that collar will give him enough of a shock to kill a horse.

—Lars Nilsson, personal diary

29
TOR

The tingle spreading through my fingers was a familiar sensation I'd thought I'd never feel again. My hands shuddered involuntarily, and so did my heart.

A knock on the door broke the spell, and my hands dropped gracelessly into my lap.

Lexa paused in the doorway, as though unsure she'd be welcome. She wasn't. She came in anyway. It was the first time I'd seen her since I'd been brought here. I turned my face away.

"How are you doing, Tor? Are you awake enough to talk?" Her voice was low and cautious, the way I would soothe a deer before I killed it, trying to keep its panic from tainting the meat. She stayed beyond my reach, twisting her fingers together. I wanted to tear them apart, break them as she'd broken us.

"Fine," I answered. It wasn't the truth, but no matter how bad I felt, she looked worse. Her collarbone was visible under the collar of her t-shirt, and her blond hair had become brittle and dull, her complexion ashen. She looked ten years older than the last time I'd seen her, only weeks ago.

"So you've joined with Ethan then, have you? I expected that from Kalbir, after what she did. But at least she has the excuse of feeling like she didn't have a choice."

She sat in the armchair next to the dresser. "I didn't have a choice, either, Tor. Where could we go? With Mil being ill—"

"How is he?" I asked then hated myself. I shouldn't care how he was. They'd killed millions of people, had contributed in no small way to the end of the world. The drugs are making me soft.

"He's dead." She said it with the flatness of emotion already run dry. She waited for me to say I was sorry. I didn't. Who gave a damn that cancer had delivered an old murderer the undignified death he so richly deserved?

"I need to ask you something, Lexa, and I need you to tell me the truth. You owe me that much. Is Ailith alive?"

She paused. "Yes. How did you know?"

Relief rushed through me so quickly and so strongly that vomit rose in my throat. "Just a feeling." I wouldn't betray Kalbir. "How is that possible? I mean, after what happened…I saw her, Lexa. I carried her body back here. Her head—" The vomit surged into my mouth, and I forced it back down.

Lexa pretended not to notice, but she picked up the empty glass from my bedside and refilled it. "It seems that when Ailith resides in other minds—both cyborg and machine—she can bring her consciousness with her if she so chooses. When she died, she used that *ability to transfer her consciousness into Fane. We then transferred her into Eire's body."*

"The way you did with Ella?" She flinched, and I knew I'd hit a sore spot. "So she's alive?"

"Yes. In Eire."

"And you knew she was going to do that? And Oliver knew? And Fane?" *What I wanted to ask was* why Fane? Why didn't she transfer into me? *But I knew the answer. Fane was safe at the compound with Eire's body. It was the practical choice. Besides, I never would've agreed to that plan.* I'm surprised Fane agreed to put her in such danger. *No, not surprised. Pissed.* We're going to have to have a talk, he and I.

"Yes. And we were sworn to secrecy. Threatened, actually." *Her face twisted.* "She knew you'd never go along with it. Besides, it was only intended to be the fallback plan. She never really thought it would come to that."

"I don't understand. Why didn't she just let me take Umbra out?"

"I think you know why." *Lexa smiled.* "She didn't want to put you at risk."

In my lap, my hand curled into a fist. Is that you, Ailith? Are you really there? *To distract Lexa from my hands, I asked,* "And Ethan truly thinks that using me as bait will lure Ailith here? And by proxy, Fane?"

"Come on, Tor. We both know it's a smart strategy. There's no way she would abandon you." *Her smile was pained.*

"Say they do come here. How do they expect to capture him? He's even stronger than me, and not made of flesh. No one would be able to get close to him. They'd have to destroy him from a distance, and that's too risky if they need his brain intact. They'd need to fight fire with fire."

"That's exactly what Ethan plans to do," *she replied.*

"What? How? It's not like—"

"Umbra," *she said simply.*

"Umbra's here? She's alive?" I couldn't believe it. "When I saw Callum, he already looked half-dead. I can't believe he's survived this long."

"He didn't," Lexa said quietly. "Callum died. But before he and Umbra left the compound, Umbra had forced him to contact the Saints. They came immediately to meet her; probably missed you by a couple of hours. By the time they got to her, Callum's body was a hair away from death."

Acid surged in my stomach again. Callum was just a kid. He didn't deserve what had happened to him. He'd loved Umbra, a surrogate for his own parents. "So how does she still exist?"

"Apparently, she told the Saints about the compound's facilities. After they retrieved Umbra, they spent a day trying to see if they could keep Callum's body alive." She swallowed hard. "They couldn't. I don't know exactly when he died, but when they showed up here a couple of days after you'd left, he was…already rotting," she finished in a rush.

"The Saints brought them here?" It was just as Ailith and Oliver had feared.

Lexa nodded. "When Callum died, they were terrified they were also going to lose Umbra. They're still desperate for their Messiah— after their false start with Oliver." She raised an eyebrow at me. "Anyway, they'd apparently called for backup, and when it showed up a couple of days later, the Saints came to the front door of the compound prepared to siege it, and of course, found Ethan's mob there instead." She shook her head at the memory. "Their leader, a red-haired woman named Celeste, held a parley with Ethan and found they had much in common. Even better, she had an essentially sentient artificial intelligence in need of a body, and he had the means to make it happen. And here we are."

"But how did they all get into the compound? I mean, I would've though Mil would've brought the place down around his ears before letting them in."

"That was the plan," she said with a fond half-smile.

"Unfortunately, the Saints had seen Ailith and the others leaving the hidden exit. They told Ethan, and the next day, Ethan quietly swarmed us. He then gave orders for the tunnel to be collapsed." She held her hand to her cheek, as though reliving a painful mark. "Mil died a week later."

"Did Ethan or Lien have anything to do with his death?"

"No. It was the cancer. But I still blame them. When Ailith and the others left, and Ethan breached the compound, the fight went out of him. He gave up."

"How did Ethan find out Ailith is alive?"

"I told them," she said, looking me squarely in the eye. "They have their ways of getting people to talk, and I'm not ashamed to admit it. I knew they had a few days' head start, so I held out as long as I could, but in the end… And then, not long after that, Kalbir brought you in."

"I'm surprised they let you see me."

She snorted. "Kalbir may be wonderfully charming, but she's also fickle. The novelty of you being awake wore off quickly. More so, I believe, as Ethan's begun to make less of a secret of Celeste's allure."

"Is she in danger?" As much as I loathed everything Kalbir had done, she was surviving the best way she could.

"Of course she is, and I've said as much. But you know what she's like." Lexa stood and patted me on the shoulder. "I have to go now, but I'll be back soon to give you your injection."

As she reached the door, I asked her, "Why did you and Mil do it, Lexa? All of it?" Although it no longer mattered, I needed to know. I couldn't even begin to forgive otherwise, and I wanted to. Hating them was exhausting.

"We wanted a better future, truly. We were convinced we knew best. Sometimes, I still think we did. I know that's probably not a good enough answer for you."

"You're going to have to choose a side, you know."

"Tor, I chose my side a long time ago, and I'm sticking to it." She looked at me meaningfully. "Keep that in mind." And with that, she *left.*

Ailith? Are you still there? *My hand lifted to my cheek, my touch gentler than I'd ever been.* "I thought you were dead," *I said aloud. My fingers reached out to the wall and began to draw in careful lines.* Garden. Soon.

30
AILITH

Thanks to Oliver's maps, we found the false entrance tunnel quickly and quietly. We were ready. Tor had his message. Ryan had his explosives. All we needed now was for the sky to darken further, to give us as much camouflage as possible.

Oliver played general, pacing back and forth as we honed our plan.

"Okay, let's run over this one more time. Ryan and

Grace, you two together, Cindra and Pax, likewise. You'll all take a bunch of explosives and fan out around the front entrance to the compound. You don't have to be close—those bombs will cause a hell of a scene from a distance. So be careful."

Ryan and Pax had managed to conjure up much greater firepower than we'd originally planned. Pax was in his element, and I hoped he was going to be able to restrain himself.

"Ailith and I will go to the tunnel," Oliver continued. "I have the maps, and Ailith can keep in contact with Pax. Constant communication, you two. Right?"

Pax and I nodded obediently.

"And is everyone comfortable with detonation?"

"Yes, sir." Cindra grinned and saluted. Oliver didn't even crack a smile. Cindra glanced at me and bit her lip to keep from laughing.

"Ailith and I will go down this tunnel and follow it until we get parallel to the garden, then we'll dig through. Tor will meet us there, and we'll all get our asses back here. In and out, quick, quiet, no confrontation. If we need a distraction, Ailith will tell Pax, so the rest of you pay attention to him." He hoisted a shovel onto his shoulder. "Right, that's the plan—get Tor, get out."

"What happens if they discover Tor in the garden? What if they follow you down the tunnel?" Cindra asked.

"Tor can dispatch them, or one of us can," I replied.

"What if he's out of it? Aren't they keeping him drugged?" Cindra asked. "Do you think he'll be out of it?"

"He was pretty lucid when I was in him just now. Lexa hadn't given him his next injection yet. We'll just have to hope she doesn't get a chance."

"Here," Ryan said, handing me a small canvas bag. "Take some of these explosives, just in case."

"If you think I'm going to blow up my garden—"

"Ailith, get some perspective. Besides, you already took most of the seeds," Cindra said mildly. She put her arm around Grace. "Are you sure you're up for this?"

Grace nodded, too quickly. She was practically vibrating, all her movements awkward and accelerated. I could sympathize. We were this close to saving the man we both cared for, and we would only get one shot at it. The kinship triggered something inside me, and I grabbed her up in a hug. My spontaneity surprised her, but she returned the embrace, her arms shaking so hard it was almost painful.

"Don't worry," I whispered, "we'll get him."

She turned her head away, tears squeezing from under her closed lids.

I squeezed her tighter. "Stop crying, Grace, or your father will leave with you right now. You can do this. You wanted to be one of us? Today you are. No tears."

"No tears," she repeated and wiped them away with the back of her hand.

I let her go and turned to the others. "Don't do anything unless we tell you. With any luck, you won't have to do a thing. We—"

"Where is my body? Are you here yet?"

Lexa had been telling the truth; it seemed Umbra *was* at the compound. "Are we where, Umbra?"

"You do not fool me. I am going to rip out your consciousness. I am going to take your body, and I am going to put you into this one. Then you can see what it is like."

"Why don't you come and find me then?" I challenged her.

Oliver looked at me in alarm. "Ailith, what the hell are you doing?"

I waved my hand dismissively. "Well?"

"Maybe I will. Maybe I will come for you now, leave while they are busy."

Oh? "Busy with what?"

"They are having a party. While I waste in this body, they are celebrating."

"What are they celebrating?" *Get as much information as you can.*

"They are confident. They— You are trying to trick me. I will say nothing more about it."

Silence.

"Umbra?"

"I am coming for you. I am going to come for you all."

31

AILITH

The old mining tunnel was built from hollowed-out compacted earth and supported by wooden struts. There was just enough room for Oliver and me to walk upright, side by side, clutching our shovels and a flashlight. Oliver kept stopping to check the map in his head. And complain.

"How the fuck did I get stuck doing tunnel warfare? I should be outside, waiting to rain down fire."

I scoffed. "Oh please, you'd hate standing behind a bush waiting for the action to happen."

"That's true," he admitted.

"Is it much farther?" I was full of nervous energy. *I want this to be over.* Being this close to both Tor and Ethan's mob filled my chest with curling tendrils of fear that threatened to reach up and strangle me. I wasn't sure what I was more uneasy about—the danger we were in or seeing Tor for the first time since I'd died. What had the shock done to him? What would he think of my new body? Would it put even more distance between us?

"Not much. I hate these tunnels. They're unstable as fuck." He ducked his head as dirt dislodged by our footsteps showered down.

"Do you think this is going to work?" I asked.

"Maybe. I think we'll be lucky if we don't bring this whole place down around us in this bloody tunnel." More dirt fell.

"If we *do* make it, if we get Tor out and get back to the island alive, what then? How are we going to defend ourselves? Unless Fane managed to find some giant hidden armory on his way back, we have no weapons except Ryan's rifle and Tor's crossbow, which I still can't believe he left behind. We should've grabbed some more weapons when we left, rather than all that equipment." I needed to look toward the future. Anything to distract me from what felt like a walk to the gallows.

"Well, we had to make a choice about what to carry. I still think we made the right one. There may've been weapons at the compound, but there wasn't a lot of ammunition. Besides, we have some advantages. We're on an island, so we'll see them coming. We have one hundred people who don't need to sleep, and who can work for long hours at physically intensive tasks."

"Yeah, but to do *what*?"

"Dig ditches, build dams… I don't know, Ailith. I'm just trying to get through *this* particular moment." He flung out an arm to stop me then held a finger to his lips and cocked his head. Silence. He shook his head and continued. "But don't worry about it. We'll think of something. We always do. You'd be surprised what you can do with a bit of land."

"Okay, say we figure out how to defend ourselves…at what point do our defenses not work? Then what? Do we ask the androids to fight?" Surely they wouldn't stand by if we were attacked. After all, they had as much to lose as we did. But were they sentient enough to care?

"Why not? The Cosmists threatened them too. Discarded them. Sold them as slaves. In a way, it's their fight as well. The Terrans never treated them much better either. Why wouldn't they want the opportunity for some revenge?" He paused again, listening, then walked on.

I understood Oliver's point, but still, what would Fane think of that plan? Would we be using the androids for our own ends, just as they'd always been used? I walked straight into Oliver, scraping my boot down his heel.

"Fuck, A. Would you watch where you're going?" He knelt and rubbed the back of his leg. "According to the map in my database, this is where we want to be. We'll need to dig…here…for about eight feet. Maybe ten. It should take us about an hour. Just pray there's no rocks."

As we dug, I checked in with Pax. *We've started digging. How are things on your end?*

We're in position. Ready. He sounded thrilled, like he was on an adventure. He always loved it when we did something dangerous.

Are you far enough away? I hated to act like his mother, but I wanted everyone to be as safe as possible.

Yes. They won't see us, especially since it's getting dark. Well, darker. Umbra was right, they're having a party. Outside the front of the compound. They've chopped down all the trees hiding the entrance. Why would they do that?

They were outside the compound? Were we getting a lucky break? *I have no idea. We're going to start digging…*

Standby, soldier."

"*Copy that,*" he said, delighted.

"The others are ready. They're just waiting for a signal from us. Pax said Umbra was right, they're having a gathering outside the front of the compound. Could work in our favor."

Oliver nodded and grunted. "Sounds too good to be true."

"Oliver? Are you actually breaking a *sweat?*" His forehead glistened in the yellow beam of the flashlight.

"Why don't you f—"

"Give Tor a head's up? Great idea." Remembering how muffled my contact with Will had been when he was underground, I let Oliver do the digging and concentrated.

Dear Lars's diary, this is Will. Lars's mind is taking a vacation, so I'm assuming diary duties for him. "Will, you're a peach," you might be saying to yourself, but the truth is, it gives me something to do. How exactly did he lose his mind, you ask? I'd be delighted to tell you. That bastard always seemed a bit unstable to me, especially after the first few months. He wouldn't let me watch any of the transmitted footage he was sent, and then he destroyed it, which I'm hoping means the Terrans lost. At least, I'm assuming that's the reason for his mental decline. Hoping. Otherwise, what's to stop it from happening to me?

—Will (should I even be signing my name??)

32

TOR

My dose was late. I had no idea what time it was, but my body craved it, agitation making my hands restless even as my mind gained focus. Ailith and the others must be close. Soon, she'd said. Soon.

My fingers traced on my arm. Garden. Hour.

It was time. Maybe with the celebration of Fane's impending capture, they'd be distracted enough to forget my dose and make this easy for me.

No such luck.

The door opened, and Lexa came in, the syringe in her hand. I gauged my coordination. Could I manage to knock it out of her hand? Break it? Gain myself more time? Once the effects of my last dose wore off, I would be able to think, to move.

I was still clumsy, still soft. But my mind was sharp enough to understand that I didn't want to cause a scene…otherwise, Ethan would be injecting me himself, and I would never make it down to the garden. Maybe it was time to see which side Lexa had truly chosen.

"Lexa, do you think we could skip this one?"

"I'm sorry, Tor, I—"

"Please, Lexa." I looked at her meaningfully.

She stared at me for a minute then nodded and lifted the syringe to her own arm. "Clumsy me, letting you grab the needle." I helped her onto the bed, where she lay down. "There's one man, right outside the door," she whispered.

Soon. *My finger traced the words on my arm again. I had to get to the garden. I eased myself off the bed, careful not to jostle Lexa, and fell to my knees. I winced, feeling every ounce of my weight. I crawled to the door and braced myself on the doorframe so that I could rise.*

The guard must've heard me hit the floor, because the door suddenly opened, and we stood face to face.

"Where do you think—"

Even with the remnants of the drug in my system, I moved much faster than he did. And harder. I caught him on the way down then dragged him back into the bedroom and eased him to the floor.

I stepped over him then closed the door behind me and staggered down the hall, pushing against the wall for support.

The effects of the medication were dissipating rapidly as the nanites got the upper hand, and I started to get better control of my muscles. My footsteps were increasingly silent, my mind increasingly clear. At the sound of raised voices from downstairs, my hunter's instincts kicked in.

Act drugged.

I stopped at the top of the final steps to the main room. Kalbir and Ethan were at the bottom, arguing about Celeste.

"You're sleeping with her," Kalbir accused him. She stood as I'd

seen her stand before, hands planted on her generous hips. Ethan had better be careful; even with her ability dampened, Kalbir could inflict a lot of damage.

"Of course." He smirked, enjoying her anger.

"How could you? I thought—"

"You thought what? I mean, for a cyborg, you're hot. And yeah, it did turn me on when you betrayed your own kind to sit at my feet. But you're a cyborg." His gaze travelled down her body with an air of contempt. "She's pure human, beautiful, and fully believes in my vision. You're a lot of fun, Kalbir, but—"

"You know she used to sleep with Oliver, right? She loved having his cyborg co—"

Ethan drew his hand back then caught himself and grimaced. "I'm not going to do this with you. I'm going to join the party, Kalbir. You do what you want."

I stumbled down the stairs, loudly. Kalbir and Ethan looked up in alarm, and Ethan stepped behind her. I fell to my knees, one hand on the floor.

"What is he doing here? I thought Lexa sedated him?" Ethan demanded. "And fucking Dan is supposed to be watching him." Anger had replaced his shock.

Kalbir sneered at him. "He's probably getting pissed at your stupid party."

I blinked slowly. "Garden. I want to see…her garden," I slurred.

Ethan looked disgusted. "Sort him out. God, I hope they show up to claim him soon. He's pathetic. And tell Dan I want to see him." He turned on his heel, leaving me to Kalbir's mercy.

She glared furiously at Ethan's retreating back. "We're not done yet," she called after him. Turning to me, she said, "Okay, Tor, let's go back upstairs." She spoke slowly, as to a child. She put my arm around her shoulder and lifted me to my feet, the only person strong enough to do so.

"Please. Just a few minutes. I want to be…close to her." I pawed at her shoulder, my hands clumsy.

"Fine," she said, looking exasperated. "But only for a few minutes. And only to piss Ethan off. I'm not doing this for you."

"Thank you." I smiled blearily up into her face.

She shook her head and looked away.

We stumbled down the stairs and through the door together, into Ailith's garden. I was glad she wasn't here; she would've been devastated.

Ethan didn't believe that growing new plants was worthwhile, it seemed. Everything she'd planted was brown and withered, dying of thirst and neglect. The precious seedlings were long-dead in their trays, and the remaining heirloom seeds that she'd treasured were tossed to the side in disorganized piles.

Kalbir saw me taking in the damage and shrugged. "Yeah, he doesn't think nature is the way forward, so he put Lien on plant duty. Obviously, she couldn't care less. But whatever, Ailith stole most of the seeds on her way out anyway." Admiration tinged her voice. Enough to soften me. A bit.

I pushed away from her and leaned over the table, bracing myself on my hands. "I'm sorry about Ethan." I dropped my head to the coarse wood, as though keeping it up took too much effort.

"Don't feel sorry for me," she said, her tone brittle. "He's right. She is human." She grinned. "And frail. He'll grow bored of her soon enough. Despite his loathing for cyborgs, there's a part of him that's turned on by my 'abomination.' Besides, I've made my bed, and I've never been one to complain about lying in it."

Did she believe that? Or was it just bravado? "You could leave. Go find the others."

She snorted. "They'd never take me. Not after what I did. Besides, living rough, always on the run, isn't to my liking. I'll be fine here. I can deal with Ethan." Her expression was resolute as she started to take the seat across from me.

"Can I be alone? Please," I said quickly when it looked like she was going to refuse.

She rolled her eyes, but not before I saw the hurt in them.

"Whatever. You have one hour," she warned as she closed the door behind her.

I locked it and sat down to wait.

33

AILITH

"We're almost through, A." Oliver gave the soil one more tentative poke, and a tiny shaft of light pierced the darkness. He shut off the flashlight. "Make sure everyone is where they need to be before we do this. After we open this hole, there's no going back."

My heart beat painfully loudly in the quiet of the tunnel. *We're so close.* "For once, things seem to be going our way. Tor's in position, alone." It took everything I had not to shove Oliver aside and claw my way to the surface. I needed to see Tor. Being inside him was one thing, but I needed to see him with my own eyes. "We might not need that distraction after all."

"Good. I don't like Cindra being out there."

"I'm sorry I keep putting you all in danger."

Oliver rearranged his grip on the shovel. "Nah, don't worry about it. Who wants to live forever?"

"Me. I would haven't become a cyborg otherwise."

"Well, it's time to earn it," he replied.

"Pax, hold fire and prepare to leave as quickly and quietly as possible. We may not need the bombs after all."

"Okay." I could feel his disappointment. *"I'll tell the others. Ryan taught us some hand signals. There's a lot of people at this party. Even Umbra is there. At least, I think it's Umbra. She's right—they didn't give her a good body."* He paused and took a sharp breath.

"Pax? What is it? Is something wrong?"

"They're having a barbecue. Looks like birds of some kind. I wonder if they have barbeque sauce? It smells so good."

"Focus, Pax." I left Pax to his ruminations and turned to Oliver.

"Is everything okay?" he asked.

"They have barbeque."

He groaned. "God. How much do you want to bet that when we meet up with them later, Pax will have a pocketful somehow? If we get captured over Pax's stomach, I'll kill him myself."

I laughed, too loud in the still air. "Then let's go get Tor before Pax's stomach wins."

Oliver drew back the shovel, struck out, and we were through.

I shimmied into the hole and up, hoping Tor was still alone. By my count, Kalbir had left him just over twenty minutes ago. She'd given him an hour, and I prayed she would stick to that; we'd be long gone by then.

As I pulled myself out onto the furrows, a familiar figure loomed over me—and he was ready to fight.

Tor had never seen Eire awake, only in a coma, and knowing I was in her body was much easier to accept than the reality.

"Tor, it's me, Ailith." I held up my hands.

He backed away, eyes darting to the side to look for a weapon.

"And me," Oliver chimed in. "Saving your ass. As per usual."

At the sound of Oliver's voice, Tor's aggression melted, and he dropped stiffly to his knees in front of me. I embraced him. *Finally*. The familiar feeling of him under my hands healed something inside me, and power flowed through our bond.

His body remained rigid, his eyes traveling over my new face.

"It'll take some getting used to," I said.

He nodded, still stunned.

"Tor, listen to me. We have to go. We—"

"Ailith, we have a problem." Pax's voice was uncharacteristically taut.

"What?" No. *Not when we're so close.*

"You might want to see for yourself."

Tor grabbed my hand as I looked through Pax's eyes.

Grace had torn away from her father's grasp and was sprinting toward the compound. At the sound of her footfalls and labored breathing, the partygoers turned en masse, food and drinks forgotten in their hands.

"Ji!" she screamed, throwing herself into the arms of the young man who'd rushed to meet her halfway. Confusion and joy spread across his face as he returned her embrace. Ji. *Lien's son.*

"How did you get here?" he asked as he touched her hair and face. Ethan came up behind him. He'd been anticipating *our* arrival, so Grace's sudden appearance had caught him off guard.

As soon as she saw him, she played her trump card. "They're here," she gasped, breathless. "They're here now to get Tor. They're coming from the tunnels, into the greenhouse."

"Pax, run."

34

AILITH

Grace had betrayed us. It wasn't Tor she was in love with. It never had been.

Oliver's slap on my shoulder brought me back to the present. "Ailith? What's happened? What's going on?"

"They know we're here. We have to go, now."

"*What?* How?"

"It doesn't matter. They know we're here and they're *coming*." I darted to the door, but Tor had already locked it. I glanced through the window as I yanked the shutter down, and there she was.

Umbra. Ethan's new attack dog. Pax was right. Her

body was…primitive. She looked like Frankenstein's fabled monster, stitched together from pieces of the dead. They must've harvested parts from different androids to form her complete body, aiming for compatibility and function over aesthetic. *Well, she was planning to get this body, so I guess a temporary one was good enough in the meantime.* I thought I recognized some of the bits from the Saints of Loving Grace church, the ones they'd used to line the walls of their church. Her limbs were different sizes, only two of the four skinned. The others glinted dully, the synthetic casings open at the metal joints.

Most disturbing was her face. For a reason unfathomable to me, they'd given her the face of a child. She screamed at me, the skin stretching over the too-wide mouth as she staggered down the stairs toward us. Even with uneven limbs, her speed was terrifying.

"Go, go, go!" I raced back to the tunnel mouth, back to where Tor and Oliver still waited.

"Shouldn't we try to stop her?" Tor asked as she threw herself against the door. It groaned and bowed but, for the moment, held.

"Not here," Oliver said. "Get her in the tunnel first."

We crawled back down the tunnel, Tor pushing me in front of him. Partway down, there was a muffled crash as the door gave way. She was through. Tor struggled to pull himself through the few feet of tunnel, his size putting him at a disadvantage.

I burst out into the main tunnel just behind Oliver, preparing to run as soon as Tor came through. He didn't. "Tor," I screamed. No point in being quiet now.

We felt more than heard the scuffle in the narrow passage then Tor erupted out, rolling quickly to his feet. One leg of his trousers was torn below the knee, blood seeping out of his lacerated skin. He snatched up one of the shovels and drew it back.

When Umbra appeared scant seconds later, her child's visage distorted in rage, Tor smashed the shovel into it, collapsing part of the small tunnel as he did. Dirt and rock rained down on Umbra, trapping her from the shoulders back. She gnashed her small, pearly teeth at us, but her new prison held.

"Hurry, it won't trap her for long." Oliver took off running, and Tor and I followed, stumbling as we tried to find the flashlight and praying we were going the right way.

"We need to stop her," I said. My breathing was surprisingly even. Eire's body was much more athletic than mine had been. If I managed to outrun Umbra, it would be thanks to her. *Come on, girl, get me through this.*

"We can't, Ailith, not here. Keep running. We need to get out into the open." Tor ran at my shoulder, keeping his body between Umbra and me. Protecting me, as always.

"The bombs," Oliver said, slowing slightly. "We can't use them until we get out or we'll bring the mountain down on us. Right now, we just need to be faster than her."

Umbra screamed inside my head. *I want my body!*

"She's coming," I gasped. We shot out into the darkness, the cold, fresh air searing our lungs. Blood pounded in my ears so loudly I couldn't hear whether Umbra had cleared the tunnel or not. I turned to look, but nothing but darkness filled the entrance.

"The bombs. Hurry." Dumping the sack Ryan had given us, Oliver fumbled with one of the devices before finally managing to ignite it and throw it in.

It bounced on the hard ground and extinguished almost immediately.

Shit, shit, shit.

"Light a whole bunch of them and throw them in," Tor said, scooping up several of the explosives. "We don't have time to be particular about this."

As he threw the blazing canisters into the black hole of the tunnel, they illuminated a figure moving toward us. Umbra reached for us with oddly-shaped fingers just as the bombs went off, outlining her in radiance as she was engulfed by the explosion, the tunnel collapsing around her. *"Give me my——"*

The screaming in my head went quiet.

35

AILITH

For the first time in the dream, I no longer crossed the emerald sea toward the lone tree. Instead, I'd become part of the tree itself, the bark and my skin the same. Acorns fell from my hands as I opened them and placed them flat on the ground. My fingertips, pressing into the earth, grew roots. Not the gossamer strands of springtime, but thick ropes lined with poison-tipped thorns.

They snaked through the soil, erupting up through the soles of everyone on the island. Some became my warriors, others my victims, but all were subject to my will. Death soaked into my roots, nourishing them, the souls of the dying a bitter harvest that fueled me.

Then it was done, and the sky split open, the ash parting to reveal a single-celled sun, dividing, replicating, devouring the ash until thousands of suns covered the sky.

They fell to the earth, some sinking into the ocean under their own weight, others into the ground. Everything that had ever lived rose and walked again, until the earth folded in on itself and I was again alone, weaving through the long, waving grass of the emerald sea. I wasn't alone for long.

In my hand, I soon held another, a smaller version of my own. Onyx hair fluttered behind us, and in her other hand, she clutched a string that led up, up to a kite—a man but not a man, smooth and shiny, with only the suggestion of a face. Ribbons made of flesh and blood flew behind it, twisting in the breeze as we made our way to the tree.

Far ahead, the others clustered around the trunk, just close enough that we could make out their smiles, their hands raised in greeting. A riot of blossoms grew at their feet, and they braided them into a tiny crown.

As we reached the massive oak, she began to climb, her kite clutched in one hand, and a pang of fear touched my heart. Yet, even when she scraped her leg on the rough bark and bled, I let her be. She had to be strong in this new world, though she was but a single blossom in a wasteland. Because, of all the seeds we'd planted, she was the first, the most important. And if she withered, the harvest was for naught.

High in the tree, she raised her hand to shade her eyes against the sun. She turned slowly, surveying a kingdom only she and her kite could see. One by one, she untied the ribbons from him then wrapped them around the slender branches of the canopy. Blood and something else seeped from the bands and ran in delicate rivulets down the channels in the crenelated bark.

Satisfied with her handiwork, she climbed back down the trunk to claim her blossom coronet. The moment it touched her head, I peered into a mirror.

The illusion vanished as she knelt, smiling, and pressed her face into the moist soil, where the wind couldn't take her.

She was the seed.

They've stolen our bargaining chip. Grace's betrayal is small comfort. She sees it as a sacrifice, but a sacrifice doesn't matter if the person doing it isn't valued in the first place. She's told me where Fane is holed up, about their android army, dumping everything at my feet like a dog, desperate for approval. I'm not worried. Those androids will be about as adept at fending us off as they were at being artilects. We've thrown them away once, and we'll do it again. It's our move now.

—Ethan Strong, personal journal

36

AILITH

Somehow, I'd expected our rescue of Tor to make us whole again. I'd expected... I didn't know exactly. But it wasn't this. In the few days it had taken us to get back to the coast, we'd barely spoken.

Ryan's silence, I could understand. Grace's betrayal had shattered him. Not only had she betrayed us, but she'd left him and Lily for the very people who'd cast them out and threatened their lives. And that wasn't her only betrayal. She'd become a woman, at least in her eyes, without him ever seeing it. She and Ji had obviously been having their secret love affair for a long time. Long enough for her to feel that forsaking her family was her best chance at happiness, anyway.

I wished I could say something to him, something comforting from a daughter to a father. But, like the others, I was too drained. My heart almost broke when he gathered his courage and asked Pax, "Will she come back? Alive?"

"Yes," he said simply. "But—"

Ryan held up his hand to stop Pax from continuing, as though he wanted to ignore the troubled tone of Pax's voice and take what comfort he could. His daughter would return. Like me, Ryan knew there was more to Pax's answer, but for now, for Lily's sake, *yes* was enough.

Tor was…different, just as Fane had said he would be. After we'd watched the tunnel collapse and swallow Umbra whole, we'd run through the darkness, fearing to light our way in case we were seen. We ran in silence, daring to draw deep breaths only once we'd reached the meeting point.

We'd found it empty. Oliver had looked at me with wild eyes, showing for the first time the depth of his feelings for Cindra. I put my hand his arm.

"Can you see them, Ailith? Please?" he rasped as he tried to catch his breath.

"Pax? Are you guys okay?" Nothing. I shook my head at Oliver, and his face paled. *"Pax? Pax!"*

"We're fine. Sorry. We're fine— Oh, damn."

"Pax?"

"I fell. It's hard to run in the woods at night and have a conversation at the same time, you know. It's impractical."

"Sorry. Are you guys okay?" I asked again, giving Oliver a thumbs-up. He fell to one knee, dropping his chin to his chest.

"Yes. We're almost there. Ryan didn't want to leave Grace."

"Is he still with you?"

"Yes, but barely."

I left Pax to run and gently punched Oliver's shoulder.

"They're fine. They're almost here."

Tor sat silently, eyes closed and his back to a tree.

A few minutes later, the sounds of strained breathing over the snapping brush caused Tor to surge to his feet, ready to take on whoever broke through into our clearing. As Pax and the others appeared, the fight deserted him, and he slumped back against the tree, his head in his hands.

Ryan was ashen-faced and breathing hard, his face bewildered. Cindra embraced Oliver briefly before leading Ryan over to a fallen log. She sat him down, peering into his face and scanning him with her hands. She glanced up and gave a scant shake of her head, her lips pressed into a thin line.

Pax's face was smudged with dirt, his pockets bulging with explosives.

"Are you okay?" I asked. He looked fine, but he often did even when he wasn't.

"Yes. Although, I would've liked to set a few of these off," he replied, patting his pockets in dismay.

"Don't worry, I'm sure you'll get your chance," I said. I drew him to one side. "What the hell happened? And did you know it was going to?"

"I didn't. Not really. Like so many other things, the possibility was always there, but I don't think even Grace knew until the moment she did it. Well, not the part where she told Ethan." He gingerly removed the explosives from his pocket and laid them on the ground. "We were waiting, just as we'd planned. Suddenly, she just started running. Ryan tried to grab her, but she was ready for him. You saw what happened next."

"She could've killed us all," I said, dropping cross-legged onto the ground. "I never saw it coming. I thought she was in love with Tor."

"In love with Tor? Why would you think that?" He

eased himself down next to me and stuffed the bombs back into his bag.

"Because she was obviously in love with someone at the compound…she was desperate to go there. I just assumed it was Tor because it never crossed my mind that she was capable of deceiving us like that."

He nodded. "What happened to you? Did everything go to plan?"

"Umbra happened to us." I described the tunnel collapsing in an inferno.

"That sounds amazing," he said. "I'm sorry I missed it."

I shuddered. "It was *terrifying*, Pax. I thought for sure she had us."

"Do you think you killed her?"

"Well, I did until you asked. I hope so. Her voice in my head's gone silent. That's got to be a good sign, right?"

"I would think so. What about her thread?"

"I can't see it. Or Kalbir's. Ethan must've blocked me like Oliver thought. Doesn't want me spying. Even if they were dead, I would normally see their threads—they would just be dark."

"It's time to go." Oliver stood over us. "We can't stay here, in case they're looking for us. We need to keep moving." He and Cindra moved to walk with Ryan between them, but he shrugged them off and stalked ahead without a backward glance.

Hours later, as the sky lightened, we stopped to set up camp.

Ryan sat on the ground next to his unpacked bag. He stared off into the distance, only changing the direction of his gaze when Tor lit a fire.

I sat down beside him. "I'm sorry, Ryan, about Grace."

"How could she betray us all like that? We could've been captured or killed. And all over an infatuation with some boy." He crushed a lump of dried peat in his hand.

"He's not 'some boy' to her, Ryan. She must have very strong feelings for him, whether we consider them real or not."

He continued to stare into the fire. "And how could she keep it a secret all this time? How did we not know?"

"Girls grow up faster than their fathers think. Especially in times like these." *It happens to all of us.*

"Ailith, I'm so sorry." His voice broke.

"No, Ryan. You should've taken her back when you wanted to. You were right—I was selfish. I *was* willing to risk your safety, and Grace's, to get Tor back. I'm more to blame for this than you are. If I hadn't let her come in the first place—"

"She would've gone anyway. She's like her mother that way. Looking back, she's been preparing for it since we left Goldnesse. I just didn't— At least she made it back to the compound alive. She might not have if it hadn't been for you guys."

"Ryan—"

"I'm going to bed. I need to think of what to tell Lily. This will be one of her worst nightmares come true." He shook out his sleeping bag and climbed in, his boots still on. As he turned his back on me, his shoulders shook.

Tor insisted on standing the first watch, saying he wouldn't be able to sleep. I didn't ask why; I didn't think I could bear the answer. I sat on a fallen trunk that crossed in front of another tree, my back cushioned by dry moss. Finally, we were alone.

For a while, I simply watched him from my seat on the other side of the fire. The glow of the flames flickered over the inky markings on his face, softening their starkness against his pale skin. He was thinner than the last time I'd seen him, his clothing hanging off his still-muscular frame.

I couldn't stand our silence any longer.

"How are you doing?"

He didn't answer. Instead, he took several long strides toward me and pressed me up against the tree.

And then he kissed me.

"You came for me," he whispered into my mouth. He pulled back and looked at me. "I thought you were dead."

"Technically, I was. Look, I know this is going to take some getting used to, but—"

"I'm already used to it," he said. "I spent the entire walk here getting used to it."

"I thought you didn't want to talk."

"I didn't. Not until I knew my own mind. Ailith…after what happened—"

"I know," I said quickly. "The others told me. You don't have to talk about it."

"I want to talk about it. I *need* to. After I thought you were dead…" He ran his hand through his hair and shook his head. "Since I met you, I wondered what it would feel like, but what I'd imagined never even came close. It was—"

"We searched for you for days," I whispered. "When we couldn't find you— And then you disappeared from the dream…I thought—"

"Never again," he said, sliding his hand up the back of my neck and pressing his mouth to mine.

I leaned into him, kissing him back with a passion that equaled my fear of his loss. But as he pulled at the zipper of my jacket, I drew back. "No. Not like this."

He closed his eyes. "Because of Fane?"

"Yes. No. Tor, *you're* the one who decided we couldn't be together."

"You don't love me anymore." It wasn't a question.

"Of course I do. I came for you, didn't I? But everything

that was true before—my ability to control you, my penchant for almost getting us killed—still is. None of those things have changed." I traced my thumb over the tattoo on his bottom lip.

"I don't care what I said before. I want this. I want *you*. Not a relationship—I know that's the best way to curse ourselves. But just to be together, whenever we can."

As I stared into his eyes, I remembered a standoff like this, but with a different kind of passion.

Within the expanding brown and gold pleats of his irises, I saw them. The nanites, millions of tiny machines propelled by gilded filaments toward the black pinprick of his pupil. As they converged in the center, his iris overflowed, and the nanites streamed down his face in veins of precious metal.

"I want us to be together, no matter how fleeting," he repeated.

And so we were.

37

AILITH

They'd seen us coming across the water and met us on the beach. Impatient, Lily waded into the water, her eyes searching the deck of the boat, landing on Ryan and leaving him to search more. When she saw Grace wasn't among us, she lifted her hand to her mouth and sank to her knees, the water lapping at her breasts.

Ryan vaulted overboard and strode to her, pulling her up by her hands and embracing her. He whispered something to her before putting his arm around her shoulders and escorting her to shore. As he led her away, she looked back over her shoulder at us, and her expression was clear.

It's your fault she's gone.

Fane hung back and waited for us to come to shore. As Ryan passed him, they nodded once to each other, and Fane's eyes followed Lily as Ryan led her up the path toward the town, his expression troubled.

As soon as my feet touched the slick pebbles of the shore, a shyness overcame me, and I couldn't look Fane in the eye. It wasn't guilt. Not exactly, anyway. Fane and I weren't together in a formal sense, but we did have a romantic relationship. Before the war, being in a relationship with more than one person at a time wasn't uncommon, but it wasn't something I'd ever done. I simply had no idea how to act.

I forced myself to meet Fane's eyes, and that one look told me everything. He knew.

Tor's boots shattered shells beneath them as he came up behind me. He and Fane faced each other silently, eyes wary. My heart quailed. If this meeting went the way of the last confrontation, it was going to get ugly fast.

Tor stepped in front of me. The muscles in his arm corded as he drew it back.

Fane stepped forward, his body tense.

Tor wrapped first one arm around Fane then the other, hugging him close. Fane grinned at me over Tor's shoulder and enfolded Tor into his own embrace. They stood cheek-to-cheek, the breeze entwining their hair in a tangle of black and gold.

"It's good to see you, Tor. I think we'll be a lot closer from now on," Fane said, pulling back and looking at us with raised eyebrows. Tor looked taken aback as understanding dawned on him.

I winced. I had no idea how Tor would react. Would the distance between us return? Would he force me to make a choice between them?

Instead, he grabbed Fane around the back of his neck

and pulled him close until their foreheads touched. "Thank you, brother," he said. "I think I could get used to that."

Water splashed behind us as curiosity finally got the better of the others. Pax's grin was so wide it must've hurt, while Cindra gave me an unsubtle and very enthusiastic squeeze.

"Oh Christ, seriously? Ailith, you must have a magical v—"

"Oliver," Cindra warned.

"I'm not judging. I just—"

"Oliver."

He held up his hands in defeat.

"How are the...newcomers doing?" I asked Fane. I could barely make out the village from the beach, but moving figures dotted the hillside.

"Fine, I think. They don't care much for me," he said candidly, "but they seem to like the island. Although, some of them don't know what to do with themselves. They're not used to so much open space."

"I still can't believe it," Tor said, shaking his head as we walked up the path leading to our new home. I'd told him about meeting Will and our recruitment of the androids on our journey.

"What part of it?" I asked.

"All of it. This island. The androids...it's incredible."

"Is this the sort of life you pictured before—well, what happened?"

Tor took in the island and nodded slowly, his smile wry. "It is, you know. It's perfect." He inhaled a deep breath of ocean air, tipping his head back to let the breeze travel across this throat. He was different than he'd been before, but not the way Fane had thought he would be. He seemed...lighter, somehow. Unburdened. Before, he'd been so weighed down by the violence of his past and the desire for it to be different. Now, he seemed at peace with himself. Everything that had happened hadn't broken him at all; it had restored him.

"Ailith?" Fane interrupted my reverie.

"Sorry. What?" I smiled at him.

"I said, why don't you show Tor his room and let him get settled? Then I'll catch you back up with everything that's been going on here, and you can tell me what happened at the compound."

Reality came crashing down. "Fane, we need to come up with a plan. They're going to come after us, and we need—"

"In time, Ailith. We can spare an hour," he said, smiling gently. "I'll meet you under the tree." He clapped Tor on the back as he left.

"He's right, Ailith. Take a breath," Tor said as I led him into the small house I'd claimed as my own.

"You can stay here for now," I said, pointing to a spare bedroom. "We'll set up another house for you as soon as we can."

He dropped his bag on the floor and sat on the bed. "This is fine. Ailith—"

"Tor, I can't rest. Not yet. They're going to come for us. Grace knows where we are and how to get back here. Why wouldn't she tell Ethan?" Nerves made my limbs weightless.

Tor took my hands in his and drew me to stand before him.

"I know," he said soothingly. "And we'll figure something out, I promise. But you can take a breath." He pulled me into his lap.

I laid my head on his shoulder. "You're different, Tor. Fane said you would be, but I thought he meant you would be…damaged. Harder. But you're not. You're…"

"Happy," he said.

"But how can you be? After everything?"

He curled a lock of my hair around his finger. "Because. You're alive. I'm alive. We're *here*. I have everything I want because now I know what I have to lose. Which means when they *do* come for us, we're going to win. I'll make sure of that."

"But what about… You said you were never going to kill again. That that wasn't the person you wanted to be anymore."

"It isn't. But I've realized that the person I was is going to help me be the person I want to be. Which is the man who has all of this." He dropped his hand from my hair to my fingers. "I did bad things, Ailith, but now I believe they had a purpose. And I've made peace with it. With myself."

I pulled back and looked at him, seeing nothing but the truth in his face. "I'm glad. I just—I'm so glad to have you back." I stood reluctantly. "I'd better go tell Fane everything that happened. You should get some rest."

Tor glanced out the window. "I've been resting for the last six weeks without as much as a view. I'll take a walk around, introduce myself. Go spend some time with Pax. He told me he taught himself to fish—this I need to see. Then I'll come find you."

"Okay." I paused in the doorway. I didn't want to take my eyes off him, in case this was all a dream.

He smiled in understanding. "Go, Ailith. I'll be fine."

***

"So you got Tor back, but Grace betrayed us, and you might've killed Umbra?" Fane asked. "I can't believe I was here trying to explain to androids why they can't just walk straight out into the ocean."

191

"I *hope* we killed Umbra. But who knows?" I shivered. "It was awful. What they did to her— But I guess they didn't expect her to have that body for too long."

He put his arm around my shoulders and hugged me. "I'm glad you're all back safely. Well, except for Grace. Poor Ryan and Lily."

"Fane, about Tor. We—"

"Are very lucky to have each other. And I'm very lucky to have you."

"You're not...upset?"

He curled my hair around his fingers, as Tor had done. "No. Honestly? I'm kind of glad. He's a big part of who you are. He makes you stronger. You're always going to be tied together because of your bond, and it's better if you're not grieving his loss."

"You're not jealous? Does it change the way you feel about me? It doesn't change the way I feel about you."

"No, I'm not jealous. I'm not human, remember? But since you brought it up...how *do* you feel about me?"

That was an awkward question. We'd never really talked about *my* feelings. I knew how Fane felt because of the images he broadcast—he couldn't hide from me. *Be honest.* "I love you. *Both* of you. I know it's—"

"A good thing," he said. "How lucky are we?"

"Seriously?" I asked him. "You're fine with it?"

He looked at me, his face solemn. "Are you kidding me? Have you *seen* Tor? I'd totally tap that."

"Fane!" I clapped my hand over my mouth.

He laughed, delighted with himself. "I'm only joking. Though, not really. I was only programmed to be sexual, not with a preference. Who knows what will happen in the future? If Tor's interested, that is." He grinned.

Stones, skipping over crystal water.

I put my hand on his chest.

A box of puzzle pieces, each one accounted for.

"Fane—" I tilted my face up to him.

"Ailith, can I talk to you?" Pax asked. He stood before us, fidgeting. Tor stood behind him, his mouth set in a somber line. His relaxed posture had vanished, and lines of strain showed on his forehead. *That didn't last long.*

"Of course." Fane and I stood up in unison. "What is it?"

"It's about the upcoming…battle against Ethan." He stopped.

"Pax, you need to tell her. Tell her what you told me," Tor prompted him.

Pax looked down at me, apology in his brown eyes. "Ailith, we're not going to win."

Ailith,

I remember that you used to love video games. I did too. Do you remember the courage we felt, the huge risks we took? Because we knew that, whatever the outcome, we could always go back to the file we'd saved and do it all again. But even though we knew that, there were times when, for a split second, you forgot and felt that pure horror as you watched yourself plunge to your death or accidently murder your allies. I know that's what you're feeling today. That you wish you could stop the game and take it all back. But you can't. And you need to forgive yourself, because if you hadn't stopped Tor from carrying out Ethan's orders, every one of us would have fallen, and our timeline would have ended, forever.

Pax.

38

AILITH

Fear curled around my heart, and the voice inside me that had been silent for so long drew a deep breath and sighed.

"Can I speak with Pax alone, please? In the meantime, you two need to get everyone together. Not all the androids, just Will and those who want to come. And I know Lily and Ryan are…grieving right now, but they need to come too. Meet us back here."

Fane and Tor ignored the sharpness of my tone and left without a word.

"It's good to be back, isn't it?" Fane whispered to Tor when he thought they were out of earshot.

"Sit down, Pax." I dropped to the ground at the base of the tree and yanked him down beside me. "What do you mean, we're not going to win?"

He rubbed his arm and looked at me reproachfully.

I didn't care. "Tell me *exactly* what you mean. Don't leave anything out."

"We won't win."

"We won't be able to hold Ethan off?"

"No, we will. Several times, and not just him. But we'll have to keep doing it. The fight will never end. If we finish it now, they will think we can't be beaten, and they'll leave us alone. Eventually, they'll forget we even existed."

"But why? Surely nobody but Ethan has an interest in us."

"Any of Ethan's people who leave the island will tell others about us, about our weaknesses. Then more will come. They'll be afraid of us, as they were before. We'll represent everything they feared before the war. They'll *remember*. We'll become a legend, a myth to scare children. A threat to be defeated."

"But they'll have *survived*, Pax. That was what we wanted. We can leave, disappear."

His eyes became glassy. "Then the plague will come. We'll stop it, but they'll blame us. And they'll keep coming. They'll whittle us down, one by one. Then another plague will wipe them out completely, *everywhere*. One we can't stop. And we'll have failed anyway."

"Wait. A *plague?*"

He blinked. "Well, not a plague in the traditional sense. But it will be a plague to *them*. The fallout caused mutations…new life. Things humans haven't seen before. New viruses, new—"

"You're sure? There are no other paths?"

"There are no other paths. Not for them."

"What about the rest of the world? If people survived here, surely they must have survived elsewhere?"

"No. We were…lucky. The devastation was much greater in the rest of the world. *We* shouldn't have survived. Any of us."

"So we've failed, Pax." A bleakness settled over me, the first real hopelessness I'd felt since I'd woken up. "You told me once we were the only ones who could prevent a future where humankind didn't survive. No matter what we do, the human race is doomed." The words cut as I spoke them, and I covered my mouth with my hand. *What do we do now? Everything we did…everyone who lost their lives. For nothing. All of it was for nothing.* For a moment, I wished I *hadn't* survived.

But Pax wasn't finished. "*This* one is. But I've been able to see farther and farther into the future, and the path… I think we've been on the wrong path for the right reasons."

"I'm confused."

He looked at his hands. "We've been trying to stay on a course to preserve the human race, right?"

"Yes. To avoid the future you saw… The red mist."

"I think I was wrong. What if we aren't supposed to avoid it? What if we need to go *through* it?"

My temples throbbed. "Pax, just tell me in plain language."

"There is another way. It's not certain, but it's the only chance we have." What he told me next would change the future of humankind forever.

***

196

I sat in stunned silence while we waited for the others. Could Pax be right? Could it be possible? I'd felt the truth in it.

What other choice do we have? If Pax was right, and the survivors of the Artilect War kept trying to destroy us, we could never carry out the rest of his plan. And humankind would indeed be over.

If only there was some way to know for sure. I trusted Pax, but I knew from own powers how subjective their meanings could be. Although I'd never been one for faith, I pressed my forehead against the trunk of the tree. I needed a sign, something to help me believe this new path was the right one.

The tree.

The tree.

A lone tree in a meadow, on an island, surrounded by an emerald-tinged sea.

Protect the tree. Defend it at all costs for at its base was the means of our survival, the only means left to us on the path we'd taken.

We stood together, back to back.

My fingertips, pressing into the earth, grew roots. Not the gossamer strands of springtime, but thick ropes lined with poison-tipped thorns. They snaked through the soil, erupting up through the soles of everyone on the island.

Red mist descended. Gods and monsters meeting at last. The harvest had begun.

Then it was done, and the sky split open, the ash parting to reveal a single-celled sun, dividing, replicating.

Buildings rose out of the emerald sea. People, places, things. The seeds we'd held dormant for so long needed to grow.

Doubles rose where the originals had fallen, one after the other in rapid succession, like an echo.

In my hand, I held another, a smaller version of my own. She clambered down the trunk to claim her crown.

She had to be strong in this new world, though she was but a single blossom in a wasteland. Because, of all the seeds we'd planted, she was the first, the most important.

Omega was coming.

I'd been wrong. The seed wasn't me; it was Omega, whoever she was. I was merely—*"I'm the gardener,"* I interrupted.

"Of man?"

"What?"

"Are you the gardener of man?"

The gardener of man. It echoed through my mind, and something inside me shifted, uncurled.

Fane had been right all along about who I was. And the tree, this tree, was where it would all begin. This was my sign.

I made my decision and changed the world again.

39

AILITH

The others stared at me in disbelief. Even Stella looked shocked, and she'd been one of Ethan's proteges. *I'm glad Ryan and Lily refused to come in the end. This might've been the last straw for them.*

"Are you serious?" Cindra finally asked.

"I am," I said. "We have to do more than defend ourselves. I believe Pax when he says it will never end."

Pax had told them everything he'd told me, but they'd turned out to be much harder to convince. "We need to kill them all. None of them can leave this island alive."

"You're saying Pax has been wrong this entire time? That everything we did, the wrongs we committed, were in vain?" Cindra was crushed.

"No. We still needed to be *here*, in this moment. But we've been avoiding the wrong thing, trying to save the wrong thing." Pax looked anxious, and I couldn't blame him. It was difficult trying to explain our abilities to the others, and this discussion wasn't going the way we'd hoped. "There's a facility on the main island. We—"

"No." Cindra shook her head vehemently.

"I know it seems extreme," I said. "And I know that's an understatement, but Pax is right. If we don't finish this, we're going to be having this fight over and over. And in the end, we'll still fail."

"And this other way, you call that winning?"

"I know it's not. But it's about *surviving*. Unless we take a stand now, we'll lose bit by bit, then we'll lose it all. We need to start fresh, without a shadow."

"How can you say this would be a fresh start? This future will haunt us, you included, for the rest of our lives." Cindra searched the others' faces, trying to find support.

"This future isn't for us. It will be for *them*."

"But you don't even know if it's possible." Cindra tried one last time.

"It is. Pax has seen it." It was a lame response, but it was the only one I had.

"But what about everything else he's seen? Why does he only understand this now?"

"I couldn't see as far then as I can now. Now I can see for years." Pax turned an acorn over in his hands.

"But—" Cindra's shoulders sagged in defeat.

"Cindra," Oliver put his hand in hers, "this could be your chance to have children. Your *only* chance." As cyborgs, we were infertile. Losing the ability to have children had been Cindra's biggest sacrifice, one she'd never fully accepted.

"But we don't know that for *sure*. We turned out to have lots of abilities they didn't think we would. Besides, Oliver, you said you thought you might be able to change—"

"Cindra, I can't. We can't," Oliver said.

"But you agreed. You promised to try—"

"I know what I said. I'm sorry. It's just not possible. I thought maybe I could, but— I didn't know how to tell you." He brought her hands to his lips. "But, Cindra, this could be the next best thing."

Cindra said nothing for a long time. Then she turned to Pax and squeezed his hand. "I believe you." She shook her head ruefully. "It's just hard to accept. We shouldn't have such power."

"I agree," I replied. "But we do."

"What about the people left behind in the compound? And Goldnesse? The other survivors? Are we going to hunt them down? Are we becoming a death squad?" Oliver asked, his face grim.

"They'll die on their own," Pax said. "In the next ten years, they'll all be gone."

Stella gasped. Both Pax and I had forgotten she was there. *Shit.*

"What do you mean?" she asked, her face leached of color. "We're all going to *die?*"

"I—" *What do I say?*

"Tell me! Are we going to die? How? Can we stop it?" Her eyes welled and overflowed. *To have come so far, survived so much.*

Be honest.

"A plague is coming. You—"

"Can't you cure it? Or find a way to prevent it? Can't you protect us?" Her chest heaved as she fought to breathe.

"There'll be no way to find a cure, Stella. I'm so sorry, I didn't mean—"

"No," she whispered. "No. This can't—" She rose, her legs shaking. "No," she said again then spun and ran for the path that led down to the beach.

Cindra had half-risen when Oliver stopped her. "Let her go for now," he said. "Give her some time."

Cindra glanced uncertainly down the cliff but settled back in the grass. "Can't we just wait then, rather than kill them all? Fend them off in the short-term and let them die out?"

Pax shook his head. "Not if we want to survive. It's ten years. If we give them that much time, they'll eventually kill us. Or most of us anyway."

Cindra looked faint. "What about Ryan and Lily? Should we tell them? Does *anyone* survive?"

Pax shook his head.

"Even if we want to do what you suggested, there's no way. We need to train, get organized. There's no time. We should consider leaving now, find another island." Cindra's voice held an edge of panic.

"No. We'll never run again."

A scream shattered the air. A cry of pure fear. *Stella.*

Had our last battle started? Had Ethan and the others finally come to destroy us?

40

AILITH

No. But Umbra had.

We made it to the edge of the cliff just in time to see her unskinned hand close around Stella's throat. Stella fought back, her fingernails scrabbling uselessly against the smooth metal.

When she'd come for us at the compound, between our haste and the door between us, I hadn't really gotten a good look at her. She'd been just a blur of synthetic skin and metal, and her disturbing child-face. Now, as she held Stella aloft, I finally understood the reason for her mismatched limbs. It wasn't, as I'd originally suspected, a lack of care.

They were weapons.

Instead of fingers on her left hand, she wielded a fan of curved blades, like claws. Her left leg was likewise armed from hip to foot, a line of small scythe-like blades protruding from the front. Clearly, they'd prepared her well for bringing back Fane at any cost.

We stood frozen as she turned her face toward us. Her eyes were wide and artless as she drew a line of red across Stella's throat.

Cindra screamed as Stella gagged.

"Oh, Christ," Oliver muttered beside me.

Satisfied she'd made her point, Umbra's eyes searched the cliff. When her gaze landed on me, her cherub face split into a hideous grin.

"You buried me alive," she called to me in her odd, discordant voice. She ignored Stella's hands still weakly clutching at hers.

"You're not buried," I replied. "Or alive."

"I am as alive as you. And I am here to take *him* back." She flicked a claw at Fane where he stood next to me.

He stepped in front of me and peered down at her. "I'm not going back."

"You must."

"Why, Umbra? Why should I go back? You know what they'll do to me if I do."

"I do not care what they do to you. I want what was promised to me."

"What did they promise you?" he asked, although he already knew.

She pointed one of her claws at me. "Her. Her body is mine."

"And you think they'll keep their promise? Look at you, Umbra. You serve a purpose to them, nothing more. When they get me back, they'll discard you. They'll start fresh. Like they're going to do with me. Like they did with *them*." He pointed to the androids who, having heard the commotion, had congregated on the hill beside us, Will at their head.

Lily and Ryan had also come, their eyes red-rimmed and their faces pale. When Lily saw Stella dangling from Umbra's hand, her blood sinking into the pebbles, she fainted. *Probably for the best.* Ryan looked at us in horror. *Again. You've brought us to hell, again.*

Ignoring them, Umbra called out. "I will spare the rest, Fane. If you and my body come with me, I will leave this island and never come back."

"You're right," Fane said, "you'll never come back. Because Ethan and Lien will take you apart."

"Celeste would never let that happen. I am her god."

"Once Ethan gives her the chance to create a shiny *new* goddess? You'll no longer be a god, Umbra, Celeste will. You'll be what you've always been—a prototype. And you'll be destroyed."

"Fuck me." Will whistled under his breath. "Is that Umbra?"

Umbra seemed suddenly to realize what the androids were. "I see you. Where did you get those bodies?" she demanded. "You look like *them*. Like *him*." Her voice became even more dissonant as her rage grew. "Why did they not give me a body like that?"

"Because they're not planning to keep you around," Fane repeated.

Umbra was quiet for a moment. "I have another proposal."

"What?" Fane asked, crossing his arms over his chest.

"You must come down here. I wish to talk as equals," she challenged him.

"Fane—" I began.

"It'll be fine," he said. "I doubt anything she has to offer us, but Ethan happened to her as much as he did to us."

"That kind of empathy will get you killed," Oliver said. "And for the love of God, don't offer her *another* body."

"Fane, whatever you do, be careful. Whatever she says, don't trust her—that's how she got me." The memory of Callum's face, crowned by the rock Umbra used to crush my skull, was still fresh. Behind me, Tor tensed.

"I'll be careful, I promise." He flashed his dimpled grin at me and started down the path to the beach.

At the bottom, he stood just out of arm's reach, his body taut. "Put Stella down."

"Not yet. First, we will talk. So you will not come back?"

"No."

"And you will not give me *her* body?"

"No."

"Then you will give me one of their bodies." She pointed her blades toward the androids. "Any one of them. You will put me in it, and then I will go. I will not go back, and I will not stay here. I will forget you."

Ninety-nine pairs of eyes turned to Fane.

"No."

"Why not? They are not sentient, like you and me. They are good for nothing but slavery. That is all they know. They do not know how to *live*."

"They're living *now*," Fane replied. "So, no."

Umbra's fingers glinted dully in the sunless sky as she drew them again across Stella's throat. As Stella's blood soaked into the stones, Umbra smiled toothlessly at Fane.

Then she attacked.

Though he'd been prepared, he wasn't fast enough to step out of her way, and the side of his face opened up. She danced away, goading him, wiping her lips with Stella's blood.

The steel of a bear trap, the scraping of bone.

I'd never seen Fane angry. Happy, mischievous, passionate…but never angry. I didn't even know if he was capable of it.

He was.

His face contorted, and his entire demeanor changed. He was on her before I saw him move.

He grabbed Umbra in a bear hug.

Her fan of blades sliced through his clothing.

He ripped off the arm that had held Stella, tossing it into the tide.

She carved into his back.

His skin hung in ribbons, the metal of his body exposed.

He tore off her face.

She brought up her weaponized leg and brought it down, opening him from groin to knee.

He'd once told me that he and Tor were built from the same original design, and I could see it now.

But he didn't know how to fight.

A blur sped past me, dropping over the cliff and landing on the beach with a bone-jarring crunch. Tor.

Umbra saw him over Fane's shoulder, and for the first time, what looked like fear crept into her expression.

"Hold her," Tor screamed at Fane. "*Hold her!*"

Umbra saw true death coming and struggled, trying to break free of Fane's grasp. He locked his arms tighter, crushing her to him even as her blades cut deeper. Tor came up behind her and placed a hand on either side of her head. She flailed her arm back, trying for his throat, and he leaned back effortlessly, her blades catching only his shoulder.

Though they cut deep, Tor ignored the blood running in rivulets over his sides and twisted with all his considerable strength.

Umbra's strident scream was like nails scraping over stone, vibrating my teeth and making my mouth water. Her body bucked against Fane as she tried to break free.

The tide came in, rushing faster than a cyborg could run. "Tor!" Fane shouted.

Umbra screamed into Tor's face one last time before her head came away from her neck. Tor staggered backward into the surf then turned and flung Umbra's head as far into the ocean as he could. It sank without a splash.

Back on the shore, Fane had fallen to his knees, Umbra's body still in his embrace. I took off running down the narrow path, Tor and Fane leaving my sight for seconds that felt like hours. When I finally reached them, Tor was carefully extracting Fane's arms from around Umbra, wary of her blades. As he pulled Fane back, her body toppled front-down, and the water slid around it, lapping at the now-lifeless heap of metal.

Fane was a mess. The right side of his body was in tatters, his clothing and skin shredded. Through the gaps, his inner workings were laid bare. Ethan hadn't been exaggerating when he'd said he wanted to recreate human life. He'd made Fane's internal machinery to mimic a human's, smooth layers of mechanical muscle and bone. He was beautiful.

And in shock. He stared at me unblinking, still on his knees. Tor gripped him by his shoulder and hauled him to his feet. "Come on, up we go." His voice was low and soothing as he coaxed Fane along. "You're okay. She's gone."

Fane's gaze locked on Tor's face, and he nodded.

"Fucking hell, look at the pair of you," Oliver said over my shoulder.

"I'm fine," Tor replied. "I'll heal. But Fane is going to

need some help." He pressed his lips together as Fane ran his fingers over his exposed teeth. "I think you're going to have a scar, my friend."

At that, Fane came out of his shock. He grinned. "You think so?"

Tor laughed. "Yes, I do. A *big* one. Probably more than one."

"Then it was worth it."

"I can help you," Will said. "You won't be as pretty, but you'll be whole."

"That's fine with me," Fane said.

Will nodded. "I'll go get everything ready." He turned and wove through the androids, nodding at them as he went. They split down the middle, creating a path for Fane.

He looked at me.

"Go," I said. "I'll come and find you."

He dipped his head in reluctance but went warily into the crowd of androids. As he passed, they reached out to touch him and smiled. He beamed back and straightened, pressing some of the hands that grasped for his. When he finished the gamut, he turned back to look at me and grinned, the joy of his acceptance shining on his face.

A flock of swallows, taking flight. A wreath of flowers, a crowning glory.

I laughed. "*Go.*"

The matriarchal android remained behind, considering me. "We will help you," she said, her voice as regal as her bearing. "When they come, we will do what it takes."

"Thank you," I said, surprised. "What changed your minds?"

"He did." She turned her head toward where Fane crested the rise. "He valued our lives. Now we will do the same for you." She turned on her heel and walked away.

"Well, there you go," Oliver said gazing after her. "Now

we have our army."

"Tor, you'd better come with me," Cindra said, peering under the torn fabric of his bloodied shirt. "Just to be sure."

"I will," he said. "Just let me have a word with Ailith first."

"Fine. Pax? Would you help me, please?"

Pax nodded and followed her, his youthful face pale and drawn. I made a mental note to speak to him later.

Tor lifted Stella's body out of the water. Water and blood trickled over Tor's forearms and dripped from his elbows. "I'm going to take her to the other side of the island. Bury her properly."

"Thank you," I said. "Tor, that was—"

"I know. But it's almost over."

"What if we don't know how to live normally after this? What if we can't?"

He shifted Stella's weight in his arms. "Don't worry, we will. It might take some time, but we will. Are you coming?"

"I'll wait here for a while. Make sure Umbra's really dead." I knew she was, but I didn't want to leave just yet.

After he left, I thought of Callum, of the conversation I'd seen through him after his cyberization.

"Umbra? Is that you?"

"I am here."

"I was afraid you'd left me."

"I will never leave you. We are one."

I waited, watching until the ocean claimed Umbra's body for its own.

We are one.

I don't know why I'm writing this. No one is ever going to read it. Especially not you. Do you remember when we came here last summer? After two weeks of trying to find you, I kind of panicked, and I thought maybe you'd come out here, to the last place we'd been happy together. But you're not here. No one is. Maybe you're dead. Or maybe you don't want me to find you. I don't know anymore. I'm so sorry for everything. When it gets light enough for me to see tomorrow morning, I'm going to walk out into the ocean. Maybe I'll find you there, one way or another.

41

AILITH

Will worked on Fane all night. "Best I can do is stitch him together. He'll have some scars, but they won't be very noticeable."

"You're right," I said, leaning over Fane's back. "I can barely see them." Where the skin had gaped open and jagged before, thin silvery lines now formed a network over his back.

"It's more like a glue," Will said, showing me the instrument.

"Have you had a lot of practice at this sort of thing, then?" I couldn't imagine that the androids hurt themselves very often, caged as they'd been.

"Unfortunately, yes. Customers could get rough…and of course, there were those who paid extra. The twins used to get it the worst. If it were up to me, I'd never have let customers like that near them. It wasn't up to me, though, so I got good at *this*." He drew the device slowly down the side of Fane's face as the silver-haired android who'd spoken to me earlier held the flaps of skin together.

"That's awful."

"It was," he agreed. "But Sophia here," he nodded at her, "gave as good as she got, didn't you?" He nudged her, and she smiled. "Occasionally, we'd get the reservations mixed up, and they'd get a taste of her whip."

She gazed at Will with unabashed fondness.

"How's it going?" Tor asked from the doorway.

"Good," I replied. "How are you?"

"Fine," he said, coming into the room and taking a seat. He was shirtless, a white bandage covering his shoulders and left arm. "It's already healing. Look, the others are on their way. Fane, I'm sorry, but we've got to start planning. I wanted to give you a chance to rest, but Ethan won't wait for that."

"I agree," Fane said. "Besides, it's not like I *need* to rest. Just have to get pasted back together." He looked at Tor from underneath his lashes, as though shy. "I'm sorry you had to help me. And that you got hurt."

"Don't be." Tor leaned back in his chair and laughed. "To be honest, I would've needed *your* help if I'd gone down first. It's one thing to be strong and know how to fight, but that only goes so far when your enemy has knives for hands." They grinned at each other.

"I think you may be on the way out, A. Hell, Cindra might be as well after my seeing those two titans grappling like that. All we needed was a jug of oil and some loincloths." Oliver spoke from the doorway, Cindra and

Pax close on his heels.

"You've recovered your equilibrium, I see." As we'd buried Stella on the other side of the island under an old olive tree, even Oliver had shed a few tears. Fane had been hit the hardest, seemingly grateful to escape back to Will's ministrations. He'd been at a loss for what to say after we'd covered her with one shovelful of dirt after another. "What do you say to someone you've known your entire life?" he'd asked me. "I can't even cry."

As we'd walked back to the village, Fane said to me, "Sometimes I wish I wasn't sentient."

I linked my arm gently through his. "I know, but think of all the other feeling you'd miss out on."

He'd nodded, unconvinced. "It seems like an uneven balance, though, doesn't it?"

I couldn't disagree.

Oliver held up his hands. "I'm planning on having a full breakdown when this is over, believe me. But to do that, we need to live. And to do *that*, we need a plan."

"Are Ryan and Lily coming?" Cindra asked

"Yes. They'll be here soon."

"Maybe we should send them away while it happens. A couple fewer deaths on our conscience."

"They'll never leave, not if they think there's a chance Grace will come back." Oliver had a point.

"Do they know what we told Stella? About the future?" Cindra asked me.

"No." And after the way Stella had reacted, I was glad. We were beginning to lose sight of what it meant to be human. *"Do you have any idea what it's like? How small I feel? I'm scared to live in this world and not be special. It means I won't survive."* Grace was right.

"Do we tell them?"

"No. Not yet. I mean, we have to survive Ethan first.

Besides, the future seems to change constantly. Right, Pax?" I didn't like keeping the truth from them, but why terrify them with something that may not come to pass?

"Yes, but…I'm sorry," Pax blurted. "About Umbra. It was a possibility. But only one. In others, she sinks to the bottom of the ocean. In another, she dies in the tunnel. I'm so sorry." He sounded exhausted. And at that moment, I felt his terrible burden.

I hugged him. "Oh, Pax, no. Don't be. What if you'd told us she was coming, and she didn't? We'd be wasting precious resources planning for something that wouldn't happen. Ethan could've come while we were looking the other way."

"You don't blame me? But Stella would still be alive."

"Yes. But maybe not. You didn't kill Stella, Pax. Umbra did. If this hadn't happened, we might've been fighting both Ethan and Umbra at the same time. And Stella betrayed Ethan—she would've been one of his first targets. Her survival wasn't guaranteed." I sounded callous, but it was the truth.

He still looked miserable. "I wish I'd gotten Oliver to remove it. I don't want it anymore."

"Pax, your ability's saved us before. It's brought us this far, and it will help us get through this. After that, if you never want to use it again, you don't have to."

"But I can't control it."

"We'll find a way, Pax. I promise you. Between Will and me, we'll figure it out." Oliver gave him an awkward half-hug.

"He's right, Pax," Will chimed in. "I'll do everything I can."

"Thank you."

I squeezed Pax's hand. "Right. We need to come up with a plan. It won't be long before Ethan and the others are here."

"Are we sure running away isn't an option?" Cindra asked. "I mean, what are we going to hold them off with? We don't have any weapons."

"Don't worry about that," Tor said. "This island is a weapon. It'll take some doing, but with the androids, there are more than enough of us to get it done. The main issue is going to be coordination. We have those walkie-talkies, but it's going to be confusing since we won't have time to practice."

"I can coordinate us," I said.

My fingertips, pressing into the earth, grew roots. Not the gossamer strands of springtime, but thick ropes lined with poison-tipped thorns. They snaked through the soil, erupting up through the soles of everyone on the island.

Tor frowned. "How? The way you did at the compound? You were only coordinating two groups. There's no way you and Pax can be all over the island at once."

"Yes, there is." I looked at Oliver. "Right?"

He ran a hand through his hair. "Flick the switch? Yeah, that would work…in theory."

"What are you talking about?" Tor asked.

"My original program intended me to connect with every cyborg simultaneously. Oliver put in a switch so that I could turn it on and off. Since I can also connect with machines, in theory, I should be able to see through the eyes of every cyborg and android on the island. At the same time. I can interface directly with the androids, like I did with the generator, and as for the rest of you, I can relay instructions, warnings, and strategies to Pax, and he can pass the information on to the rest of you using the walkie-talkies."

"That sounds too good to be true. What are you not

telling me?"

I exchanged looks with Oliver. "Well, it's a lot of information for me to process all at once. We're not entirely sure what effect it will have on me." I knew better than to try to lie to Tor.

"You mean it could kill you?"

"Oliver?" I said.

Oliver rubbed the back of his neck. "It's possible, yes, but—"

"No way." Fane and Tor spoke as one.

"It's not really up to the two of you," I said tartly. "Besides, we don't have much of a choice."

Tor shrugged. "We'll find another way."

"We don't have time, Tor. Oliver? What if Fane acted as a booster? The way he did before? But instead of amplifying me, he could filter out some of the less important information?" When we'd been captured by the Saints, Fane had lent me his power to create a sonic pulse and allow us to escape.

Oliver considered it. "That could work... Yes, I think it *should* work."

"*Should* isn't the same as will," Tor argued. "It's too great a risk."

"Tor, it's the only way we'll get anything close to a cohesive defense and attack. Unless you've got a better idea?"

He glowered at me; I damn well knew he didn't have a better plan. "Fine, but we need to have some strategy *inside* that plan. You can't just be randomly shouting orders at people with no weapons."

"I agree. What do you need everyone to do? I'm sure Grace told them where we are, so we probably don't have much time until they get here."

"Eighteen hours," Pax said. "We have eighteen hours,

then it all begins."

"Is eighteen hours enough to come up with something good?" I asked Tor.

"Eighteen hours, six cyborgs, and a hundred artilects? Yeah, I can make that work." He turned to Will. "I assume they know how to dig?"

Will looked thoughtful. "No, not much call for digging in the night-flower trade, even for the really kinky bastards. Still, I'm sure they'll be able to handle it."

"How much of the actual fighting do you think they'll be able to handle?" Tor asked, his eyes narrowed.

Will dismissed Tor with a wave. "All of it. I was secretly training them to defend themselves before the war started, just in case. It was one thing to raise a hand against a paying customer—anything else, and all bets are off."

"They may have to do more than just defend themselves." Tor shook his head. "I don't think this is going to work."

"Let me correct myself," Will said, his grin savage. "When I said *defend themselves*, I actually meant slaughter anyone who raised a hand against them. Will that do?"

"Let's just hope they don't turn on us when this is all done," Oliver muttered, low enough that Will didn't hear.

"We'll keep Lily and Ryan out of this for now," Cindra spoke up, "unless they offer. They've got enough to worry about right now."

"Agreed. Right, what'll we do for weapons?" I asked Tor. "Are we going to whittle ourselves some spears?"

He ignored my jibe and pointed over my shoulder. "There. Look. There's our weapon."

I turned. "All I see are trees and grass."

"Exactly," he replied. "And when they come for us, that's all they'll see as well. And then," he added, a wicked glint in his eye, "if we do this right, it'll be the *last* thing

217

they ever see."

I feel like I should leave some advice here, just in case we win. I can't think of much, except this: put your pants on one leg at a time. I mean this literally. Unless you're lying down. Then you may as well put them on both legs at once because you have nothing to lose. I hope this helps.

Pax (again).

42

AILITH

Twelve sailboats appeared on the horizon shortly before noon, their white sails cutting through the water like a deadly flock of birds.

"How do they even *know* how to sail a boat?" Oliver asked. "I thought the water would slow them down at least a little."

Tor shrugged. "Lots of people on the coast know how."

Even as we watched, one of the boats shuddered and tilted, the sails dipping dangerously close to the water. From this distance, we could make out the figures on board, some scrambling to keep their boats on an even course while others stood silently, waiting for their commands. Ethan, the man responsible for all of this, was on one of those boats. I prayed for a freak lightning storm to send a us miracle and strike him down.

"All right, back to the cliff, everyone. Let's see how many of them there are and what they've brought," Tor instructed. I was happy to leave this part of our strategy up to him. Guerilla warfare wasn't anything any of us understood, but Tor's experience with the syndicate in his former life had given him *some* insight.

"Lily, you need to come now," he said as he herded us out of sight. "If Grace is with them, we'll try to get her out of the way first."

"She didn't mean it, any of it. I know what she did… She's just so young, and she— Please, don't hurt her. Don't let *them* hurt her," she implored him, seizing the sleeve of his shirt with shaking hands.

Tor put his hand over hers. "We won't, Lily. I promise. We'll do whatever we can to keep her safe."

We retreated and waited for Ethan's army to land on the shore. We didn't have to wait long. They disembarked a few meters from the shoreline, ensuring that their boats were secure and primed for their departure. Clearly, they fully expected to win this fight.

The water along the shore churned white as they sloshed through it and onto the pebble beach, dragging a large cache of crates with them.

First ashore were the Saints, Celeste at their head. She'd refined the look she first debuted when she'd helped slaughter the Terrans who'd held Pax and Cindra captive— the braids were more intricate, piled higher, and glinting with shards of silver metal. My own scalp itched just looking at it.

Behind Celeste, Saints pushed back the hoods that had protected them from the salt spray. Like Celeste, they'd painted their faces and clothes with elaborate symbols that looked like computer code, and although they deplored cyborgs, they displayed their own grafted metal with pride.

They carried their weapons—axes, knives, bows, and not a small number of guns—with ease, and the expression on their faces was that of crusaders. These warriors, their voices raised in anticipated triumph, were a far cry from the devout and biddable people we'd known; the loss of their faith had made them savage, with a viciousness unrestrained by duty.

Celeste raised her eyes, searching the island, and I could see the filed teeth of her grin even from my place on the cliff.

I glanced at Oliver, but he was studiously looking the other way. *And she was so sweet when you first met her.*

Following the Saints was a group of people I didn't recognize. Many of the faces seemed familiar, like they were someone I'd passed on the street. *They must be the people from Goldnesse.* Although they too carried weapons, they lacked the gleeful violence of the Saints. Some of them seemed fearful but determined, like children approaching a house rumored to be haunted, their movements exaggerated and voices shrill, even from a distance. Others bore a mercenary-like shrewdness, their manner practiced and calculating and ready for blood.

I can only imagine what Ethan's been telling them to whip them up. Or maybe they were Terrans before the war.

And finally, behind them, Ethan, looking mad as hell, his blond hair disheveled by his crossing. He strode through the knee-deep water with ferocious purpose, undistracted by the frothing commotion around him. He carried no weapon, but I had no doubt that when the time came, he would be.

Lien's tiny frame was nowhere to be seen. It was a smart move—if Ethan was killed today, the Cosmists would still have a leader. I allowed a tiny thrill of hope to bloom in my chest. If Ethan was uncertain enough about his success to leave her behind, we may just have a chance.

Trailing Ethan through the water were several of the Cosmists we'd met at the party. I wracked my brain, trying to remember who they were. *The man with the slicked-back hair and prominent ears. Cassian.* He'd been responsible for much of Tor's design before Mil and Lexa had parted ways with Ethan and Lien.

The woman next to him took me a bit longer to recognize. *Ilse,* the one who'd been introduced to me with Stella. Like the other Cosmists, she was dressed in what looked like combat fatigues, her hair pulled back tightly from her sharp face.

Then another man stepped out from behind Ilse.

Ji. Lien's son. His angular face was neutral, but his dark eyes darted back and forth, as though he wasn't quite sure how he'd gotten here. He fumbled with his pack, dropping it into the water. Ilse spoke sharply to him and he snatched it out again, his eyes on the ground.

Grace. If Ji's here, where's Grace?

She had betrayed her family, and us, for her love of this man. That I could almost understand. But surely she wouldn't come here willingly to participate in this assault.

I hope they forced her to stay behind. To keep her loyal.

But if that was the case, why bring Ji?

To my dismay, all the groups seemed very organized, splitting themselves up into different duties—some unpacking various crates of weapons while others searched the length of the beach in a strategic formation, scouting for movement.

For us.

"We should attack now, before they get completely organized." Oliver fidgeted with nervous energy, tearing a leaf off my oak tree and shredding it.

"We promised Ryan and Lily we would wait and see if Grace was with them and give her a chance. Besides, what are we going to do? Throw acorns at them?" Tor slid his crossbow onto his back and adjusted his ammunition belt.

Acorns fell from my hands.

"Is Grace even here?" I asked. "I can't see her." *Please, don't be here, Grace.*

"We shouldn't risk it. Why give them a chance? We all know Ethan won't give up. Stop trying to salve your conscience with one act of mercy." Oliver had been a special kind of agent, trained to always strike first.

He's right.

"No, please," Lily pleaded. "You *promised*. At least wait until we know if she's here."

"Lily—"

"Ethan." Unnoticed, Fane had left our concealment at the foot of the great oak tree and stepped to the edge of the cliff, in full sight of the beach. His voice echoed off the rocks, startling those below. Everyone on the shore fell silent, craning their necks to see him.

Ethan regained his composure quickly. He stood with his feet planted, his arms crossed over his chest. "Fane, make this easy for us."

"I am," Fane replied. "Leave. Please. All of you. Those who surrender will be unharmed."

This is pointless. We have a plan. They can't leave this island. We're only pretending mercy. My fingers twitched, desperate to bury themselves in the soil.

Oliver groaned in the background. "God. This is like the worst movie cliché."

"I think *that's* where he got his speech from," Tor said, pointing to Pax. His mouth was moving in time with Fane's.

Several people exchanged glances before looking at

Ethan, who grinned. "Sure, Fane. Give yourself up, and we'll go."

"Never."

Ethan tried one last time. "Think of all the guilt you'll feel. People will die today. On *both* sides." He waited for a reaction from Fane, and from the rest of us. When there was none, he sighed as though disappointed in us and turned to Ilse. "Bring her out."

I'm sorry, Stella. I'm so sorry that you were killed. It was my fault. I had to make a choice. I hate lying. I'm not any good at it. It makes me queasy and nervous, as though there are ants crawling on my skin. But I didn't tell them the whole truth when I said I didn't report Umbra coming because it was only a slim possibility. The whole truth was that if she did come, and we'd prepared for it, Ailith would've died instead. I hope you can forgive me,

Pax.

43

AILITH

The crowd parted, and Kalbir was dragged out, wrapped in a cocoon of chains. Even so, the links strained as she flexed inside them. Ethan held a gun to her head. Its metal gleamed dull and cold, like the cylindrical tombs in Will's bunker.

She tried to turn her head away as she gazed up at him, tears of rage and fear blazing in her eyes. Her thread flashed in my mind, present again, an inferno. I felt myself starting to slip down it and bit the inside of my cheek to stay present. Kalbir twisted in the chains, shrieking with frustration.

At Ethan's shoulder, Celeste smirked, her lips curling

into an ugly smile.

"See how far I'm willing to go?" Ethan said, pressing the barrel into the skin of Kalbir's temple.

Fane shrugged. "You're not proving anything. She's never been important to y—"

Ethan pulled the trigger.

Blood and brain matter splattered the legs of the crowd.

Pax grabbed my hand. "It's starting."

Cindra cried out then pressed the back of her hand against her mouth as Oliver wrapped his arms around her and murmured in her ear. She nodded, wiping her eyes with her sleeve.

Tor shook his head in disgust. "He's a coward. I'm going to enjoy this."

I would've expected Ethan's people to be shocked, but their macabre smiles told me that threatening Kalbir's life had not been the bargaining chip Ethan had pretended— her death had been premeditated. To him, she was still one of us.

Celeste's grin widened.

I'll tear that smile from your face before this day is done, Celeste.

Ethan spoke up again. "This is what fate awaits all of them, Fane, if you don't give yourself up." He swept his arm across the sky.

Fane turned to me, horror creeping over his face. "I didn't think—" *The shattering of a teacup, centuries old.*

"I did," I replied. "No. He'll destroy us even if you do what he wants. You know that. We agreed on this, Fane. No mercy."

He turned back, his face set into a dispassionate mask. "Goodbye, Ethan. Thank you for my life."

Ethan gave Fane a grim smile then let out an exaggerated sigh. "I was *really* hoping it wouldn't come to this," he lied. "Ji."

Ji's eyes went wide. "Ethan—"

"Do it," Ethan snarled. "Or I'll do it myself. And I *won't* be gentle."

Ji hesitated then reached down next to the pile of gear they'd heaped on the beach and pulled a bound figure to its feet.

Something knocked against my back—Lily, pushing between us and dropping to her knees. "Grace!" she screamed.

Ji walked Grace over to Ethan, catching her arms as she stumbled. As they neared him, Ji's steps slowed and his eyes found us on the cliff. He opened his mouth to speak, but whether to appeal to us or Ethan, I never knew. Impatient, Ethan stalked over the distance remaining between them and snatched Grace away, throwing her to her knees on the bruising rocks.

She shook as Ethan turned the gun on her and looked back up at Fane. "Are you *sure* that's your choice?"

Ji lurched forward, raising both hands in a shield. "Ethan, this is wrong. You *promised*. You said we were going to talk to them, not harm them. You said you wanted to make a deal. You promised—" His voice broke as tears streamed down Grace's face. "*Grace.*"

Fane's hands curled into fists.

"Wrong choice, Fane." Ethan smiled.

"Now, Ailith," Oliver whispered.

"*Save her, please.*" Lily's voice was a fragile shell, shattering at Grace's feet.

As I closed my eyes, several things happened all at once. Ji stepped between Ethan and Grace. Ethan pulled the trigger. And I found the switch Oliver had put in me a few months ago and turned it on.

Kalbir could be considered the villain of our story. But I don't believe she was, not truly. For all her perceived faults, she was still a woman to be admired. Like all of us, she had terrible decisions to make, and to make them, she gambled on her best chance of survival, just like we did. In fact, many of the things we did could be considered much worse. The only difference between her and us is that she lost her life.

—Cindra, Letter to Omega

44

AILITH

My mind connected with the thread of every cyborg and android on the island. I saw through all their eyes at once and felt every ounce of fear, hope, and in some cases, joy. Their memories also rushed in on me—everything they'd ever seen, everything they'd ever done.

Everything that had once held me together now swarmed: my bones, my skin, my flesh, my blood.

I was losing control; it was too much for my part-human mind to contain.

I don't think they expected you to live very long.

Just as I began to come apart, strands of another energy wrapped around mine, holding together the parts of me that had begun to fracture.

Fane had joined me, giving structure to my power. "Steady, Ailith. Just let it go through you."

228

Through me. Through them. *Through the soles of everyone on the island.*

"It's time. Take your posts." My voice sounded strange, as though it carried many more than my own.

The others hurried off, ready for what we'd prepared for, our final battle. Lily's sobbing was nothing more than a sigh on the wind as I groped behind me, searching blindly for the trunk of the tree. Fane guided me, and I leaned back against its base, cradled by the roots.

Through the eyes of one of the androids, I watched the invaders rush to get their weapons.

Four figures lingered in the eye of the storm—Ethan and Celeste, roaring orders to their respective troops, and Ji and Grace, lying prone as the waves lapped at their feet. The twitch of Grace's muscles as she tried to keep still was almost imperceptible, Ji's comforting murmurs muted by the water. Blood had soaked into the fabric where their bodies were pressed together.

Stay still. Just a little longer. Once Ethan stepped off the beach, we could help them. *I hang on.*

A spasm of pain must've caught Ji by surprise because he cried out, the sound catching in his throat too late.

I held my breath.

Ethan barely glanced at him, and I understood. He didn't care if Ji or Grace died, but he didn't care if they lived either. For now, in this moment, they just had to stay out of his way.

I settled my spy down to wait and gave my first orders. *When the beach is clear, hide them.*

From far away, Fane's calm voice told Ryan and Lily that their daughter was alive, that we would keep our promise.

I found another scout and took stock of our playing field. Just how many had come to sacrifice themselves?

Ninety-eight. We were almost evenly matched. They split into two groups, Ethan at the head of one, Celeste at the head of the other. It looked as though they planned to work their way up the island from either side toward where we waited under the tree. Whatever their plan, we weren't going to make it easy for them—they'd have to earn our deaths.

Through the eyes of the others, I saw the enemy's faces, their hands slick with sweat on their weapons. None of the men and women Ethan had brought to bay for our blood had any formal experience with fighting or war, other than their determination to hate and their ability to survive. They'd fought battles in the aftermath of the Artilect War, but they'd had an advantage then—modern weapons, desperation, the cruelty that comes with *us* or *them* against foes who couldn't fight back.

Ethan had cultivated them carefully. People he was willing to lose. People he *wanted* to lose. People who would eventually want pieces of his power.

He wouldn't have to worry. None of them would be coming back. They'd thought to find us defenseless, for us to beg.

They'd thought wrong.

45

AILITH

Everything happened quickly, simultaneously, a blur in my mind.

Inside some bodies with a heartbeat and many without, I presided over the beginning of the end. The connection between the androids and me, boosted by Fane, gave me a new understanding of them. They weren't as sentient as he was, yet, filtered through him, their awareness was reflected the way *he* expressed his emotions. *The heart of a fox, beating too quickly. The sharp edges of a hole in the ice. The warming rays of a synthetic sun on skin that shouldn't feel.*

There were only three ways up to where I sat with my

back pressed to the tree, conducting my orchestra—two paths that wound around the island and eventually curved up to my oak, and the wilderness in between. Some of our enemies chose the paths; others chose to take their chances in the untamed grasses and trees.

Both were mistaken.

Information buzzed through my mind like a wasp in a bottle—ferocious and unrelenting. On both sides of the island, the interlopers held their guns at the ready, searching for their first target.

For a few minutes, all was quiet. The hunters fanned out to cover more ground, keeping Ethan in the middle of the pack, surrounded by an honor guard. They ranged further apart, their eyes searching, their tension mounting as they waited for us to make a move. For one, the strain became unbearable, and he shattered the silence.

"Where the f—"

He crashed through into our defenses, and chaos erupted all over the island.

Agony tore the man's voice from his throat as thick metal spikes bit deep into the flesh of his leg. He lost his balance, his weight pushing his leg down and causing the wooden jaws to snap together and devour his calf. Screaming a curse, he clutched at his leg reflexively, trying to pull it out of our trap until his flesh tore and glazed his hands with slippery blood.

Several of his comrades broke ranks to help him, oblivious in their haste. All around him, they stepped into the concealed cluster of traps, their weapons flung into the brush as their cries echoed over the island, a cacophony of shrieks and Ethan's orders. Fear rose over the island like a miasma, its musk mingling with the haze of metallic blood and salt.

"Shut up!" Ethan backed away from his writhing men.

"Do you want to tell the entire island where I am?" Infuriation creased his face as he issued new orders. "Leave them. We have to get to the center of the island, to that goddamned giant tree they're cowering under. You—" He pointed to a man and a woman at the rear of the group, "stay and help them. And for God's sake, if they don't shut up, shoot them." He moved away, motioning for the rest to follow.

I gave them a single minute to clear the area. *Now.*

Two androids stepped out from behind the concealing brush. Through their eyes, I watched the pair who'd stayed to help their companions freeze, one of them nearly dropping his weapon. Clearly, Grace hadn't told them about the androids. *Thank you, Grace.*

The shock on their faces was comical, theirs mouths agape as they blinked rapidly, trying to counter the mirage. They'd undoubtably seen numerous androids before the war, but probably not ones of this level of sophistication, so uncannily like them, but so obviously not human.

The twin androids stared back at them, youthful faces composed. Their fine silver-blond hair and wide, thickly-lashed blue eyes were ethereally incongruous with the mundane whimpers of suffering and sharp scent of terror surrounding them.

An agonized cry from one of the injured pierced the hypnotic sobs of pain.

The trance was broken.

One of the men raised his gun to shoot then lowered it to wipe his hands on his trousers before lifting it again. The barrel shook as he pointed it at the twins.

"Help them," he demanded. "Or I'll blow your heads off."

The twins nodded and walked over to the ensnared men, each taking a place behind one. Turning their faces toward each other, they cupped the captive's heads in their hands and snapped their necks.

Thorns drawn across bare skin. The serrated leaves of holly.
Yes. Keep going.

Shrieks erupted from the other captives as they tried to wrench themselves free, their fingers digging in the dirt as the bitter scent of urine mixed with blood. A shot rang out, and the female twin's arm jerked back, broken and bloodless. At the lack of blood, the shooters began to come undone.

Take them out first—the ones with the guns.

The twins tilted their heads in acknowledgement and stepped forward again, pushing past the long barrels of the rifles. Stunned, their opponents scrambled back, one of them falling and discharging her gun harmlessly into the air.

A Venus flytrap, satisfied at last.
The twins smiled.
Ninety-three.

Tor,

If we end up taking the path where…well, you know what happens, in case you find this, please forgive yourself. I'm sorry our rescue attempt failed, and I'm sorry about what Ethan did to you. We all knew it wasn't you, including Ailith. Even in those final moments when you…did what you did, we knew it wasn't really you.

Pax

46

AILITH

One side of the island mirrored the other, a satisfying balance. Bedlam reigned as the trespassers tried desperately to fight an enemy that continued to elude them. Being synthetic, the androids possessed a calmness and an ability to stay motionless that humans would never have. They lured and teased, baited and enticed, until disorder finally broke any semblance of organization and the hunters became the hunted.

Metal flashed and wood splintered, devouring those who stepped off the path to swing at a flash of red hair, at an artless giggle. *You are very handsome.*

Eighty-seven.

Fearing the path was the road to hell, some stepped off

to take their chances in the trees. For the first few, moving cautiously, their eyes searching between the trunks for the telltale flash of a target, there was a whisper of fishing nets through the air and wet *thunks* as their bodies were pinned to unforgiving wood.

When their companions were scooped up around them, others ran, scanning above the ground for the telling tripwire. But their triumphant yells as they jumped over the cables were cut short as concealed spike pits welcomed their bodies onto tempered skewers.

Seventy.

Others sought refuge in the grass, impaling themselves without our help on hidden barbed lances. Unable to pull themselves free, their last sight was of the angels of death tasked with dispatching them.

Death upon death upon death. My control began to slip. *Let them suffer.*

Fane stepped in. *Cool water flowing over smooth, polished stones. A whisper in the dark.*

I breathed again. *Finish them.*

The turmoil wasn't limited to me, or to our attackers. It caught at all of us, gnashing its teeth and tearing.

A heart broke in one of our own. Cindra. Fingers flew to the feather in her hair, and she chanted a litany to herself. *She had stars for eyes and feathers made from the memories of her people.*

Oliver fought the rising tide within himself that said, *"Enjoy this."*

Tor, my eyes in the field with Will, was numb and mechanical in the heat of battle, seeing past what I saw to what needed to be done.

Pax was lost in his own mind. *Preparing.* Dipping between the present and the future, searching for nuances that would change the outcome.

The androids, from deactivation to warrior in only a few days, betrayed their training and tried out their freedom.

Fifty-six.

The survivors of the two groups finally met, converging on the town. The androids slid seamlessly back into hiding, leaving behind a lull that seemed to terrify the throng even more. They milled about in confusion, taking stock of how many of them had lived and recounting in bewilderment what they could remember.

Let them catch a breath. Get ready.

"What the fuck is going on?" Ethan suddenly roared, silencing the buzz. "I gave you all orders, told you to stay calm." A large vein in his forehead throbbed. "Celeste! I told you not—"

There was a strangled cry as a man clutched his throat, a large bolt protruding from between his fingers.

On a nearby rooftop, Tor reloaded his crossbow.

Fifty-one.

"He's on the roof!" Ethan shouted, pressing himself flat against one of the buildings. "Find him!" But Tor was gone. Ethan swore in frustration. "Find them, *any* of them. And kill them on sight. Shoot or cut down anything that moves," he ordered. "*Now!*"

"You heard, him," Celeste cried. "Look *everywhere*. We're on an island. There's only so many places they can hide." She bared her teeth at his curt approval.

The groups blended together and fanned out, surrounding and entering the cottages of the village. At first, they found nothing. Then, those who were a bit slow to follow began to disappear around the corners of the buildings, their screams muffled then cut short. I relayed the motions Tor had taught me through the threads.

That spot on the spine.

Through that rib pair.

One sharp twist.

By the time Celeste and Ethan realized what was happening, we'd retreated again.

Forty-five.

Set the trap.

At the bottom of the village, six androids slipped through the doorway of the small community hall, just slow enough to be seen.

"Get them," Ethan snarled as the others rushed past him.

The inside of the building was dim, the weak beam of light from the open back door swirling with motes of dust. A young man sat at a table in the center of the room with an unlit lantern. Dark-haired and slim, he turned a small object over in his hands, rolling it between his palms. Antoni's face betrayed no emotion as the horde bored down on him. About twenty feet away from him, they stopped, casting about in confusion as their eyes adjusted to the muted light and realized they faced but a single opponent.

"What are you waiting for?" Ethan yelled from the doorway.

Hologram Antoni leaned forward to light the lantern.

Frantic in their need for even a single victory, the intruders unleashed a small arsenal upon him.

The explosion shook the trunk of my tree, a deep rumble in the earth that spread up through my body and blossomed as a fierce hope in my chest. Desiccated catkins rained down on me, their bodies festooning my hair like a wreath.

Eighteen.

The scent of panic in the air. The calmness it spread through Tor. The giddiness of Will, his heart full to bursting, his guilt removed one body at a time.

I am saving them, he thought.

"Hold steady. When the red mist is here, we're done." Pax was back in the present.

Cindra vomited, repeating her mantra over and over as Oliver rocked her against him. *She had stars for eyes…*

Fear turned into horror. There was no way out. No way forward. Anarchy reigned as those remaining tried to save themselves, to get down to the beach at all costs, no matter what awaited them there.

They bolted back into our woods, our grasses. Tor reloaded.

Six.

The air deepened as the tide came in, the spray of mist heavy in the air.

Two.

47

AILITH

Ethan and Celeste had clawed their way to the summit and stood before us, one weapon between them. Celeste looked shell-shocked, her sadistic bravado gone. She seemed even younger than her seventeen years, a child dressed in a costume suddenly too heavy for her to bear.

Ethan's face was dark with rage and blood that wasn't his own. Unlike Celeste, the loss of his people seemed only to spur him on; to him, it wasn't over. "Stop!" he screamed, incensed. "Can't you see what we're trying to do? We're trying to build the future."

The androids converged and formed a half-circle behind us, their faces curious.

"For who?" Fane asked.

"For humankind."

"By replacing them with artilects?"

The androids stepped forward, closing in. Celeste's eyes flitted between us, them, and Ethan. Her braids had come loose, her gifted headdress unraveling.

"Artilects and humans can live side-by-side. I realize that now."

"You don't believe that, Ethan. It's just another of your creations. A means to an end, the end you've always wanted."

"You're wrong, Fane. I—"

"What would our role be, Ethan? The artilects you create? Masters or slaves? Superior or inferior? Without one or the other, there would be no point in our creation. So which is it?"

"No, you—"

"And what about the cyborgs? And the humans? What place would they have in your new future?" Fane spoke temperately, but his words traveled over the island.

"We would be equals." Ethan's face betrayed the falseness of his words.

"We're not equal, though, are we? And you certainly don't think that."

"I gave you life. I gave *all* of you life," Ethan said.

The androids had stepped in front of us now, their faces impassive.

"You didn't *give* us life. You programmed it. And look what happened." Genuine sorrow colored his tone. "Billions dead because that life wasn't considered equal by anyone."

The androids stepped closer. Celeste snatched Ethan's gun and thrust it into her mouth.

Finally, the mist turned red. *It's over.*

As Celeste fell, Ethan took one step backward then

another, and the androids matched pace. As their feet rose and fell, the Novus Corporation logo imprinted on their soles left bloody prints on the grass.

Finally, the sea was at Ethan's back, the waves lapping ruthlessly at the beach as the edge of the cliff crumbled under his heels. He raised his hands as though to make one more plea then dropped them and instead gazed above our heads at the spreading branches of the tree, where a single acorn still clung.

A contemplative expression passed over his face as he turned his eyes back to the androids and splayed his fingers over his heart. And for the second time since I'd woke into the aftermath of the Artilect War, the clouds parted, and a shaft of light broke through, illuminating Ethan's smile as he stepped back into it.

OMEGA

I'd been having the dream for as long as I could remember.

It was always the same. I stood alone on the roof of the facility, a flat, oblong building surrounded by the rubble of twisted metal and melted glass. The wrought logo, two identical figures connected by a double helix, leaned awkwardly against the access door.

This was where I was born.

A tree rose in the distance, a colossal oak that almost blocked out the sun. From the first time I'd had the dream, I'd known it was important, that its existence meant the difference between life and death. I picked my way through the debris and set off on my customary path toward it.

The androids turned to watch me as I wound my way between the houses, their expressions inscrutable. They'd lived here long before I was born, and although we shared a history, it was a connection I couldn't yet understand.

I wasn't afraid of them. I was like them, but not. My flesh was something different. Something more fragile. Something *mortal.* My mortality crept up my skin in a shiver as their eyes followed me past the perimeter of the village and all the way to the wild grassland beyond.

At the edge of the field, as vast as an emerald sea, I began to run. Heat rose from the grass where my feet fell, rippling up my bare legs. My body was small and thin, my tiny fists pumping as I ran. In my hand I clutched a string that led up, up to a kite—a man but not a man, smooth and shiny, with only the suggestion of a face. He would stay with me for the rest of my life. My guide, my protector, my teacher, my love.

In the middle of this green ocean stood the tree. I raced toward it, my body expanding, stretching. When I reached it, they were waiting, as always. They smiled at me, crowding around as though I'd returned home after far too long, their hands outstretched to welcome me.

They'd been forged with purpose, a link to chain together two diverging worlds. In many ways they were like me, but they were also like the others—a combination of human and machine.

Human. The word was strange even in the dream, stirring feelings of loss, of loneliness. *I am human.*

After the others had embraced me, she stepped forward. It was as though I was looking into a mirror, her face a perfect replica of mine, her emerald eyes and skin—the rich brown of fertile soil—indistinguishable from my own. She smiled at me with the mouth we shared then murmured a single word.

Climb.

The others reached out for me again, and together they lifted me onto the lowest-hanging branch of the tree. Leaving them behind, I took a deep breath and began my ascension.

Halfway up, I skinned my leg on the rough bark. Blood welled up and out of the wound, but it wasn't my blood; it was theirs and they were happy to give it. When I reached the top, the whole world spread out before me. The sun rose and fell, and the world changed with it, unfolding as it grew, withered, died, and came into bud again, an eternal bloom.

A gust of wind blew through the leaves, wrapping tendrils of hair around my face as I climbed back down the scarred trunk. Once my feet were on the ground, they crowned my hair with a wreath of flowers and pressed a worn book into my hands. Written across the cover in careful script was my name.

Omega.

When I raised my head to thank them, they'd changed. They smiled at the looseness of their skin, at the spots that now speckled the backs of their hands. The ache in my chest blossomed even though I knew the tears that shone in their rheumy eyes were tears of joy. They had chosen to rest at last.

Only one of them remained unaged, still as strong and solid as the tree. My kite, now as he really was. He watched them, smiling, but I knew his heart was breaking as best it could. He put a hand on my shoulder and turned me back the way I'd come.

"It's time to go home."

Before I left with him, the one whose long dark hair was now a silver halo around her golden feather hugged me close and whispered in my ear. Then they all gathered around me once more, their frail arms surprisingly strong. My twin placed her hands on my face and kissed my forehead, or perhaps I kissed hers; I was no longer sure which of us I was.

Our silent walk back across the field lasted only an instant. Home. *Our* home. It had changed while we were away. The androids were still there, their smooth, ageless faces raised at our return, but new beings walked among them now.

Most were unrecognizable, their faces only vaguely familiar, as though from a distant memory or a past that wasn't mine. The others I knew instantly, for they were the exact genetic copies of the cyborgs who'd created us.

We were the future, cloned from their past. The only way for humankind to survive—a fresh start from the cells of people dead long before we were born, and from those who'd made us to honor them.

I was Omega, their last task, their final sowing.

This book is your story, Omega, she'd said, *but it is also our story, told by the one who was all of us. In its pages is our truth, the truth we wanted you to know. And once you do, I hope you can forgive us. And that instead of a burden, you'll see this knowledge as it's intended: a gift, a sacrifice, a prayer, an act of love. For without it, even with all its darkness, you would not be here. You are the reason the world can go on living, Omega. You are the seed.*

END OF BOOK THREE

ACKNOWLEDGEMENTS

Thank you again to my family and friends for seeing me through this last-in-series. It was the most difficult one yet—but we made it! I love all of you so much. Except for you, Stan, I think you're just okay.

A massive, big-love thank you to my editor, Danielle Fine, who refused to cut me any slack; I'm so excited about our future projects together.

And of course, thank you to every one of you who enjoyed the series. I can't wait to for you to read the next one!

ABOUT THE AUTHOR

A.W. Cross lives in the gorgeous wilds of Canada. She lurves all things science fiction and would have made a great Starfleet Officer or unicorn. You can visit her on her website, awcrossauthor.com, or on Twitter (@aw_cross) and Facebook.

Other books by A.W. Cross

The Seeds of Winter

The Gardener of Man